LOVE IS A RAINBOW

Harriet was looking for love. Deep in her heart was the memory of Jeremy, her sweet and innocent first love. She had been badly hurt by him, and it seemed she might never inspire deep and lasting love in any man. When opportunity offered she went to London to snatch with eager heart the attentions of two very different men, believing that love is a rainbow, a promise of lasting happiness. But a promise is not always kept.

JULIET GRAY

LOVE IS A RAINBOW

Complete and Unabridged

LINFORD
Leicester

First published in Great Britain

First Linford Edition
published 2000

British Library CIP Data

Gray, Juliet, *1933* –
   Love is a rainbow.—Large print ed.—
   Linford romance library
   1. Love stories
   2. Large type books
   I. Title
   823.9′14 [F]

   ISBN 0–7089–5644–0

Published by
F. A. Thorpe (Publishing) Ltd.
Anstey, Leicestershire

Set by Words & Graphics Ltd.
Anstey, Leicestershire
Printed and bound in Great Britain by
T. J. International Ltd., Padstow, Cornwall

This book is printed on acid-free paper

1

Harriet woke to the bright rays of sunshine streaming across her bedroom. She threw back the covers and padded on slender bare feet to the window. Opening it wide, she knelt on the cushioned window-seat and lifted her face to the warm sun and the blue sky. For days it had been raining . . . a steady, cheerless drizzle which had begun to get on her nerves. But at last the sun had shown its face once more and it was a beautiful morning.

The birds were singing and the tall trees were heavy with their summer foliage and the garden was filled with the scent and prettiness of the flowers which opened their faces to the bright sun. The marmalade cat sat in the middle of a flowerbed, delicately washing behind its ears.

It was a beautiful morning. The

peace and beauty of her surroundings wrenched suddenly and unexpectedly at Harriet's well-trained emotions for this was the last time that she would kneel on this familiar window-seat to greet the new day. For she could no longer look upon Calderwick House as her home.

She had woken in this small room beneath the eaves for the first time as a seven-year-old child. She had played under those tall trees with her dolls and games . . . a quiet, docile little girl. She had sat beneath their shade with her books . . . an earnest, dutiful schoolgirl. Older and expected to make herself useful, she had spent hours on her knees weeding the flower-beds. The sleek and supercilious feline who washed himself in the middle of the pansy bed had been a tiny, playful, orange ball of fluff such a short time before . . . now he was an elderly cat, Harriet thought ruefully. Ten years had slipped away so swiftly . . . and dragged so interminably.

She knelt on the window-seat and looked at the garden and in her mind's eye she saw the shy and bewildered little girl who had first been brought to Calderwick House. She had been seven years old and it had been too difficult to grasp that Mummy and Daddy had gone away for ever and she would never see them again. Sent out to play while the grown-ups talked, she had stood in the garden, clutching her doll, staring at the square, neat house while the square, neat windows stared back in most unfriendly fashion and Harriet wondered why she had been brought to live in a house that did not like children.

She soon discovered that it was Aunt Sarah who did not like children . . . Aunt Sarah who seemed so old to a little girl. She was old, of course, even then . . . too old to take kindly to the disruption of her life by a small child. An indomitable old lady with a will of iron and a strong sense of duty, she had made herself responsible for

Harriet simply because there was no one else able or willing to provide for her. And she had provided all that a child could want . . . a comfortable home, toys and games and books, clothes and shoes, a good education. Harriet had learned to be grateful for the kindness and generosity which led an elderly invalid to take on the burden of bringing up a child who had very little claim on her . . . and she had been still a child when she realized that one day she would be expected to repay all that generosity in some way. For several years she had devoted her adult life to recompensing her great-aunt for all that she had done.

Sarah Burns had always enjoyed ill-health . . . and at times, Harriet thought wryly, that enjoyed was the operative word! For her great-aunt's primary concern had always been the state of her health. She had been delicate as a child and she had been swift to perceive the advantages of invalidism. Small bones and a deceptive fragility of build and looks had given her an appearance of frailty that protected her from many of the unpleasant facts of life. She had been cherished by a doting father for many years and she had been wise enough to realize that a husband would not be so patient or so tolerant of her delicacy . . . and so she had never married nor wished to marry.

She had been content to spend her entire life in the small, quiet village, knowing little of the outside world and almost indifferent to its existence. A private income had allowed her to live comfortably and to occupy her time with books and music and painting and embroidery . . . and when she exerted herself sufficiently to offer a home to the little daughter of her favourite nephew, killed so tragically with his young and pretty wife in a rail disaster, it was in the comforting awareness that her very capable housekeeper would take over the actual duties involved in caring for the child. For at her age and with her heart in its precarious condition no one could really expect her to look after a little girl herself!

Harriet brought her thoughts back to the present and moved away from the window. Taking up her robe, she slipped her arms into it and tied the sash firmly about her slender waist. She sat down before the dressing-table and took a long, hard look at herself . . . and the clear grey eyes in the mirror looked back without flinching. Grey eyes that were fringed with thick, long lashes . . . grey eyes that seemed so clear and candid and yet had so often concealed the thoughts and emotions of a girl growing into womanhood in the narrow, restricting confines of life with an elderly invalid.

She studied her face dispassionately. She had good bones and good skin and a healthy complexion. Her nose was simply a nose with little to recommend it. Her mouth was a trifle too large, a hint too generous with its full underlip . . . it was a sensual mouth and sensuality was very much out of place at Calderwick House, she thought wryly. On the whole it was a sensible, well-behaved face that had been schooled for many years not to betray the passion and rebellion that lived in her heart.

Long, pale hair fell to her waist, thick and waving, gleaming in the bright sun . . . a woman's crowning glory and her only beauty, Aunt Sarah had always declared with a hint of satisfaction. On leaving school, Harriet had wanted to cut her hair. The heavy plaits were an irritation and fashion decreed short, almost boyish styles that year Aunt Sarah, horrified, had instantly forbidden her to follow a ridiculous fashion that would deprive her of her one beauty . . . Harriet had protested, even daring to point out that at seventeen she was old enough to decide for herself — and Aunt Sarah had promptly fallen back on the familiar threat of a heart attack. Harriet had submitted, later admitting to herself that it had been rebellion rather than a real desire to lose her lovely hair which had prompted that short-lived defiance.

Aunt Sarah's heart had given little real trouble throughout the years — but it had been a useful trump card to produce whenever anyone threatened to thwart or inconvenience or displease her. And Harriet had not always been the tractable, self-effacing, dutiful young woman she was expected to be in view of all the kindness and generosity bestowed on her. She had been quite rebellious at times, in fact — and there had been one unforgettable day when she had actually expressed a desire to leave Calderwick House and lead a life of her own. Aunt Sarah had immediately suffered a severe heart attack which Harriet privately thought had been more alarming for the old lady than anyone else!

Harriet had wished to be married — the unforgivable sin, apparently. She had been nineteen at the time . . . a slender, almost pretty girl with the pale hair curling softly about her shoulders and grey eyes large and luminous with loving. Jeremy was very handsome with his laughing dark eyes and his ready smile and his brisk confidence. She had finally found the courage to mention their engagement to her great-aunt. The subsequent heart attack had been quite genuine and Aunt Sarah had almost died. Dr Fraser had warned Harriet that the old lady's heart would not tolerate another such attack and he did not expect her to live much longer in any case. Harriet had resigned herself to nursing her great-aunt for the time being. But Jeremy was young and impetuous and impatient and he would not or could not accept that her first loyalty must be to the old lady who had given her so much through the years. They had quarrelled. It was their first quarrel . . . and their last. Within six months, Jeremy had married Dr Fraser's pretty daughter — and Aunt Sarah, clinging grimly to life, had made a remarkable recovery.

Eligible men were few and far between in the quiet little village and so it was not surprising that no one had taken Jeremy's place in her life. She stared at herself in the mirror. Her eyes were clear and bright. Her skin was smooth and fresh and still young. Her hair was thick and vital and shining with health. But her youth was slipping away, nevertheless. She was twenty-five . . . and she yearned for the romance and adventure and excitement that she had been denied throughout the years.

It was six years since she had cried herself to sleep night after night over Jeremy . . . and she had known for a very long time that she had never really loved him. She had simply been desperate to love and be loved and eager to snatch at the promise of freedom from the bleak and narrow and demanding life that she led with her great-aunt. She still thought about Jeremy from time to time and even allowed herself to be a little sentimental about the brief happiness they had known with each other . . . and it was still a comfort to remember that one man had loved her and wanted to marry her even if he had been little more than a boy, even if his love had been short-lived and too easily discouraged.

Harriet twisted her hair into its usual knot on the nape of her neck, securing it firmly. Then, still in her dressing gown, she went down the narrow staircase to prepare a frugal breakfast for herself.

There was little to do before she left. The house was clean and tidy and she had packed most of her things before going to bed. Harriet stood in the large and inconvenient kitchen, nibbling at a piece of toast and sipping her coffee, thinking of the past and refusing to worry about the future.

It was months since she had thought of Jeremy but this morning had brought him vividly to mind. She did not really regret the way things had turned out. The occasional, inevitable meeting since his marriage had never caused the slightest pang or made her heart beat even a little faster. But she did regret that it was probably too late for her to hope for marriage with any man. For she did not have youth or looks or money or social standing to recommend her — and the kind of life she had led all these years, so quiet and sheltered and dull, had not fitted her to hold her own in the outside world. Her social life had been virtually non-existent and she had very few friends of either sex. Aunt Sarah had never approved of the kind of people that Harriet had instinctively liked . . . school-friends had never been quite good enough for Harriet, adolescent friends had jarred the old lady's nerves and sensibilities too much, new acquaintances — particularly male — were never quite suitable for one reason or another. Harriet was kept too busy with looking after Aunt Sarah and running the house to accept many of the invitations that came her way — and eventually, inevitably, there were fewer and fewer such invitations.

Soon after the end of her schooldays, her great-aunt had begun to complain of a dwindling income and rising costs . . . and very shortly afterwards, just as though it had been arranged, Mrs Jessop announced that she was leaving to live with a sister who was crippled with arthritis — and Harriet discovered that it was her duty to take the elderly housekeeper's place and lessen the burden on her great-aunt's purse. She had rebelled — but only in the privacy of her own room. For what choice did she have? Aunt Sarah had fed and clothed and housed and educated her for over ten years and she was entitled to some return for all that she had done for a mere great-niece . . . and Harriet had tried to ignore the cynical suspicion that it had all been done with this very outcome in mind!

Aunt Sarah had been determined to live to ninety at least . . . and she must have been furious to be thwarted by a superior will. For Harriet had taken a tray of early morning tea into her great-aunt's room one morning — and brought it out again untouched. Dr Fraser had arrived promptly in response to her summons and confirmed that the old lady had died peacefully in her sleep. Regarding the frail little figure in the massive bed, Harriet had marvelled at the indomitable will that had kept her great-aunt alive so much longer than anyone could have anticipated.

It had taken her a little time to realize that Aunt Sarah's death meant that she was free to live her life as she pleased . . . and now, three weeks later, she was still not used to the sudden change of her circumstances. How she had ached to be free when she was younger! How she had rebelled against the dictates and demands of the autocratic old lady who had shaped her life just as she wished all these years! Now she had her freedom . . . and did not know what to do with it.

For one thing, there was no money . . . or very little. And she could no longer rely on having a roof over her head. Aunt Sarah had been a proud and secretive old lady and she had never discussed her financial affairs with Harriet except to complain that she could not continue to meet the rising prices and that they must practice further economies. Harriet had always been told that the house would belong to her eventually and she had been led to believe that there would also be a sum of money that, properly invested, should provide her with a small but adequate income. Therefore it had been a most unpleasant shock to learn that the house had been sold over three years before when Aunt Sarah's money had finally dwindled to nothing. It had been sold with the unusual proviso that she should continue to occupy the house during her lifetime — and thus sold at a ridiculously low price and the money, instead of being invested, used to pay all the household bills in the past three years so that there was nothing left for Harriet but a few hundred pounds.

It was enough to keep her while she looked for a job. It would be more difficult to find a new home. But she was fortunate . . . a friend from her schooldays had written to her with an invitation to share her flat in London while she looked for a job and a flat of her own and Harriet had gratefully accepted. She was not sorry to leave Calderwick House . . . it had been her home for eighteen years but it had never been dear to her and she could leave it without a pang. Indeed, she was looking forward to living in London and enjoying a different way of life, to seeing places and meeting people, to standing on her own feet and relishing her independence at last . . . and she was young and feminine enough to hope that love and happiness might be waiting for her somewhere in that unknown future.

At midday she was due to hand over the keys of the house . . . and then she would really be free. The morning passed very slowly. She took a leisurely bath and dressed carefully in the fashionable navy and white check suit that was the first thing she had actually bought for herself with money that she could call her own. She wore her hair in its usual thick knot on the nape of her neck . . . but she abandoned the pale lipstick that Aunt Sarah had approved for a new vivid colour with more than a hint of orange which seemed to emphasize the coolness of her ash-blonde hair and the warmth of her sun-kissed skin and the clear brightness of her eyes.

Harriet packed the last of her personal possessions and carried her cases down to stand in the hall. She made a brief tour of the garden and said goodbye to Duke who had long ago made his second home with a neighbour and would not even miss her. Then she made a final tour of the house, checking each room carefully, thankful that the heavy oak furniture which she had polished for too many years would no longer be her responsibility. Aunt Sarah had sold certain pieces of furniture to the buyer of the house and Harriet suspected that he had acquired some valuable antiques at bargain prices but she did not really care. She had been made to feel too often that she was dependent on her great-aunt's charity to have the least desire to benefit from her death. The remainder of the furniture was to be sold and Aunt Sarah's solicitor was making arrangements for the sale and Harriet would receive a cheque in due course.

She was a little curious about the new owner of the house. She imagined he had bought the place with the intention of selling it again at a considerable profit in due course. She had not met David Mellish but she could not suppose he had bought the house for his own use. What kind of man would want an old house in a quiet village where nothing happened but births, deaths and marriages — and very few of the first and last these days as the young people deserted the village for the new housing estates nearer to the thriving market town of Cashing?

Aunt Sarah's solicitor had called on her to explain how matters stood and to assure her that she would not be hustled out of the house and Harriet had gained the impression that the buyer of Calderwick House was a personal friend of Andrew Preston. She had also received a brief, kindly letter of condolence from David Mellish which contained an assurance that he was in no hurry to take possession of the house and she must feel free to take as long as she wished to make arrangements for her future.

Harriet had been impressed by the kindness of a stranger who could not have foreseen that it would be more than three years before he could take possession of the house he had bought from an ailing old lady. She was looking forward to meeting David Mellish. But it would be a very brief encounter for Rae was driving down to take her and her luggage back to London and they were due to lunch with Rae's parents in Cashing before leaving for town.

As the minutes ticked steadily away, her heart began to pound with excitement. For very soon she would begin a new life and she could scarcely wait to close the door on the past . . .

2

The house sat in its neat surroundings in the village street. A small, square house of red brick which had mellowed to russet with the years. Long, latticed windows with the green shutters set back against the walls. A quaint little porch jutted out unexpectedly from the front door and virginia creeper nestled gently about its wooden sides. The garden was well-kept and massed with flowers.

It looked very much as it had looked on that summer day three years before when he had known that he wanted to own it. He was not a sentimental man but he had known immediately that the house could be home to him and that he could find peace of mind and content beneath its roof. He had felt the house to be the fulfilment of a dream he had cherished for many years . . . a dream of living once more in the quiet village where he had been born . . . the only child of the parish vicar and the well-known novelist that Guy Mellish had met and so unexpectedly married in a matter of weeks.

David had spent his boyhood in Calderwick and carried many memories in his heart and mind of the place and its people. He had been just twelve when his shy, gentle father died from a neglected cold which turned to pneumonia and David was taken by his mother to live in London. She returned to a way of life that marriage and motherhood had interrupted . . . a way of life that David instinctively loathed but learned to accept.

He was sent away to boarding-school and his attractive and very clever mother had more time to write the books that were considered dangerously outspoken then but would not raise a single eyebrow now . . . and more time to spend with the friends who were extravagantly *avant garde*. She soon married again . . . and divorced that husband to marry for a third time. Her books were bestsellers and she enjoyed her life to the full after the years she had spent in a quiet village. A teenage son was a slight embarrassment. But David grew up rapidly . . . and soon he was at University and making something of a name for himself there, beginning to write in his turn and meeting with a success he had not dared to anticipate. He married, seeking the happiness and stability of home and family that he had not known since childhood . . . but his wife was a journalist who put her career before domesticity and did not want children. After the inevitable divorce, David did a great deal of travelling and a great deal of writing and almost forgot the long-cherished dream of living in Calderwick.

But he ran into a cousin he had not seen for years . . . a cousin who was a solicitor with offices in Cashing, the busy market town just a few miles from the village where David had been born. Talking idly and not very seriously of his dream of buying a house in Calderwick one day and settling down to write his long-delayed masterpiece, he was taken up quickly by his cousin who promised to look out for a suitable property. Only a few weeks later, Andrew had contacted him . . . and sent him to look at Calderwick House.

David had been dubious. He remembered the place which was not exactly the cottage that he had in mind. He remembered, very vaguely over the distance of twenty-odd years, that it had been owned by an elderly woman who was seldom seen and rumoured to be a witch by the village children. He was surprised to learn that she was still living for she had seemed old and very frail all those years ago. He remembered that there were other houses in Calderwick that would suit him very much better . . . but those properties were not on the market. Nor was Calderwick House . . . but

Andrew had assured him that the old lady was willing to sell at a very low price if she could occupy the house for what remained of her lifetime and he had pointed out that David was in no particular hurry to move down to Calderwick and that Miss Burns was very old, very ill and in very straitened circumstances. He had inherited her affairs from his father and did not doubt that Miss Burns would take his advice in the matter.

David was not too sure that it would be a sensible step . . . until he saw the little house set back from the main street in its beautifully-kept garden and knew he wanted it and must have it even though it might be years before he could actually call it his home.

It had been just over three years, in fact . . . years that had passed very quickly for a man who was much in demand for lecture tours and literary lunches and writers' club meetings, worked steadily at his books and lived a full social life besides. There were so many demands on his time that it no longer seemed such a good idea to make his home in a quiet village forty miles from London and all his many commitments. But as a weekend retreat or as an escape from the city during the summer months it might prove to be very useful and convenient.

He had still not decided when he drove down to Calderwick that morning in late May. Andrew had informed him of the old lady's death some weeks before and spoken of a niece who had lived with Miss Burns and looked after her and suggested that she might need a little time to adapt to her altered circumstances and dispose of various of her aunt's effects. With little interest in a middle-aged woman he had never met and with no pressing need to take possession, David had agreed that it was unnecessary to hustle the poor woman out of the house immediately after the funeral.

Earlier that week, Andrew had telephoned to tell him that the niece was leaving the house on the Thursday and handing over the keys at the same time. His agent's illness had meant the cancellation of an appointment for lunch on that day and so David had decided to meet his cousin at the house to discuss the necessary work to be put in hand. He left London early and enjoyed the drive into the country. The sun was shining for the first time in days and he liked to think that it was a good omen for the future.

He arrived in the village just before noon and parked his car in the forecourt of the pub that stood just across the road from the house . . . the pub that he would learn to think of as his local, he told himself with a faint glow of satisfaction.

He went in and ordered a lager and was pleased to discover that it was just as cold as it should be. He exchanged a few pleasantries with the landlord without assuaging the man's obvious curiosity about a stranger in Calderwick and then he took his drink to the window that overlooked the street and the house.

He gazed at the house — his house — with appreciation. There was much to be done to it, of course . . . repairs and alterations and improvements. There would be carpets and curtains and furniture and household essentials to buy. His shrewd cousin had seen to it that some of the old lady's furniture was included in the price. Andrew was an enthusiast about antique furniture but David was much more interested in the house. The house was really very charming — and he was ridiculously excited about walking into it for the first time as its owner. His home, he thought with rare sentiment — and just a stone's throw from the Vicarage where he had been born. It had taken him over twenty years to come back but he had kept the promise he had made to himself as a twelve-year-old boy!

It had helped that Miss Burns recalled his father. It had helped that she did not approve of towns and cities and applauded his desire to return to the country. It had helped that he was a famous and very successful writer and she was not above being impressed by the fact although she had never read any of his work. It had helped that he had made a good impression on the old lady when he looked over the house and tactfully refrained from talking about the alterations and improvements he would eventually carry out. There were other properties in Calderwick and no doubt a suitable cottage could have been found for him . . . but from the first moment of seeing it again he had known that it must be Calderwick House for him . . .

With an unfamiliar feeling of proud ownership, David gazed at the house . . . and suddenly the front door opened and a young woman appeared. She stood by the porch and lifted a hand to the leaves of the virginia creeper. Then she walked slowly to the gate . . . a tall, slender woman in a fashionable suit. David felt a prickle of curiosity.

She was young and attractive and there was something about her, some indefinable quality, that attracted the interest of the man who liked the company of women but had steered clear of deep emotional involvement since his disastrous marriage. He set his empty glass on the nearest table, nodded to the landlord and stepped out into the sun.

The girl stood at the gate, scanning the street as though impatient for someone to arrive. David, watching her, wondered . . . some friend or relative of the niece, perhaps — or someone from Andrew's office, stepping into his cousin's shoes because of some last-minute crisis?

Suddenly she glanced down at her feet . . . and a slow, sweet smile illumined her face. She stooped to scoop a large, marmalade-coloured cat into her arms and straightened as David reached the gate.

'He's a beauty,' he said lightly, admiringly. He added, smiling at her startled expression: 'May I introduce myself? I'm David Mellish.'

Harriet had expected him to arrive with the solicitor. Moreover, engrossed in the cat, she had not seen his approach. 'Oh . . . ' She hastily set Duke on the ground and brushed a few strands of fur from her fingers. 'How do you do?' She gave him her hand very briefly. 'Do come in . . . ' she exclaimed in slight confusion, opening the gate.

David passed through the gateway and closed the gate behind him, mentally noting that it needed attention. He bent to stroke the cat who arched its back and stared at him frostily and then stalked off in arrogant disdain. David straightened, smiling. 'I'm afraid I didn't make a very good impression.'

'Duke dislikes strangers on principle,' Harriet explained. She smiled a little shyly at the man who was not at all what she had expected. For one thing, he was quite young . . . in his middle thirties, probably. He was tall and very good-looking with dark, crisp hair that waved back from a lean, angular and very intelligent face. Meeting the very blue eyes that crinkled when he smiled, she decided that his letter had not misled her . . . he was a warm, kindly man who really cared about people. She went on lightly: 'Isn't Mr Preston coming, after all? I mean . . . am I to give the keys to you, Mr Mellish?'

David stared at her in surprise, rapidly erasing the mental image he had cherished of a downtrodden, middle-aged spinster who had been dependent for years on an old lady's charity. 'But . . . surely *you* aren't Harriet Burns!' he exclaimed in disbelief.

'Yes, I am.' Harriet smiled, much amused, swift to perceive that she did not compare with the mental picture he had formed of her . . . just as he was very different to the elderly, dignified scholar she had visualised since learning that the new owner of the house was a writer. 'I'm sorry . . . I should have introduced myself immediately.'

'But I expected — I mean . . . '
David broke off, a rueful smile lurking in his eyes. 'You're much younger than I imagined,' he said simply. 'Miss Burns was such an old lady . . . '

Harriet nodded. 'I think you must be confused about the relationship, Mr Mellish. Miss Burns was my great-aunt — and she was old when I was born!'

'My cousin didn't make it very clear,' David said slowly. He was surprised that Andrew had not thought to mention the youth and attractiveness of the niece who had lived with Miss Burns. He was relieved that she was young and obviously healthy for it had pricked his conscience at odd moments that he was the cause of turning the poor dear out of her home. But this confident young woman was surely quite capable of standing on her own feet . . .

'Your cousin? Mr Preston? I was not aware . . . So that's how it came about!' Harriet said impulsively, a little tensely. 'I wondered how Aunt Sarah thought of selling the house on such unusual terms! I suspect she was cleverly persuaded into selling at all, in fact . . . she was very fond of this house and it held many memories for her!'

'You didn't approve . . . ?'

'I knew nothing about it,' she exclaimed with a hint of resentment. 'I only learned a few weeks ago that the house had been sold — over three years before! Quite frankly, I feel that your cousin should have told me at the time!'

'Perhaps he thought that you knew all about it,' David suggested reasonably.

'I suppose so. But my aunt was a secretive woman . . . and I expect she thought I might leave her if I found out what she had done.'

'And would you have left her?' he asked quietly.

Harriet hesitated. 'I still don't know,' she admitted frankly. 'I've asked myself that question so many times . . . and I just don't know. She was very good to me and I owed her a great deal. But it was still a mean trick to serve me after all the years of telling me that the house would be mine eventually — and she allowed me to think that till the end!'

'I'm afraid you are upset . . . and with good reason, apparently,' David said with concern.

'Oh, I didn't want the house!' she said swiftly and with conviction in her tone. 'I had every intention of selling it as soon as possible, anyway. It makes things easier that I don't have to find a buyer or worry about disposing of all the furniture . . . but the money would have been useful, I must admit. However, it was Aunt Sarah's house and she had every right to do as she wished with it. For my part, I shall be very glad to leave Calderwick House!'

'I'm sorry that you haven't been happy here,' David said quietly, turning to look at the house which seemed to him to smile a welcome.

Harriet was astonished. 'Why should you care?' she demanded . . . and the words sounded a great deal ruder than she had intended.

But he was not offended. He looked at her, smiling a little quizzically. 'I don't know . . . but I do. It seems such a pity when I'm sure the house was meant for love and laughter and light hearts . . . '

'Perhaps it was . . . a hundred years ago when it was built! But it's a long time since there's been any of those things beneath its roof!' she said with feeling.

'Then I must see to it that they come back to the house,' David said firmly.

She stared at him. 'Do you mean to live here?'

'Yes, indeed . . . some of the time, anyway. I travel a great deal and I have to be in London for various engagements but I intend to make the house my home.'

'I hope you will be happy here,' she said politely — and a little dubiously.

David chuckled. 'But you don't think I will be? Wait and see! By the time

I've let in some light and air and got rid of that depressing dark paint and introduced some new ideas on decor and furnishings you won't know the place!'

'I don't suppose I shall ever see it again,' Harriet returned coolly . . . and turned at the sound of a car which slowed as it approached the house. 'Here is your cousin . . . on the stroke of noon,' she said lightly as the church clock struck the hour. 'He's very efficient, isn't he . . . likes everything just so and exactly according to plan.'

Her tone did not convey approval and as she moved towards the gate to welcome his cousin David was struck by an odd similarity in her wary attitude to the cat who had resented his attentions. She did not exactly spit or arch her back . . . but it was very obvious that she did not like Andrew. And, watching as Andrew got out of his car and held out his hand to Harriet Burns, he realized that it was a mutual antipathy. Of course, if she blamed Andrew for talking the old lady into selling the house over her head and let him know her feelings in the matter then it was not surprising that they had no liking for each other.

He believed her claim that she had not wanted the house which obviously held no happy memories for her. But no doubt she had banked on getting the house on her great-aunt's death and selling it for a very high price on the open market . . . and in three years property prices had rocketed! The old lady had been in straitened circumstances at the time of the sale and no doubt had needed the proceeds to live on and there could not be much left of the cheque he had given in exchange for the house and furniture. It was very possible that Harriet Burns had been left with nothing. She was young and obviously healthy and intelligent and no doubt she would either find herself a well-paid job very quickly or find herself a husband in the shortest possible time. It would be quite ridiculous for him to feel the slightest degree of responsibility for a young woman he did not know.

But he liked her. She was direct — and he liked that. There was a great deal of character in her face — and he liked that. She was a mature young woman of charm and intelligence and warm personality — and he liked her. It seemed a pity that they would probably not meet again once she handed over the keys to the house and went away to lead her own life in very different surroundings.

But perhaps she had friends in the village and would visit them from time to time. Perhaps they would meet again one day . . . and he would enjoy showing her a very different Calderwick House and proving that it had no need to be dark and dismal and depressing. The house had much to offer . . . it only needed love and attention and interest to create a warm and welcoming atmosphere within its walls . . .

3

Andrew Preston was tall and dark. He was also very good-looking and Harriet fancied that he was aware of the fact and traded on it. She did not know him well and she did not like him, thinking him arrogant and insensitive. He came down the path to greet his cousin with apparent warmth of affection.

'This is quite a day for you, David,' he said. 'A day you've dreamed about for more years than you care to remember, I daresay.'

David thought the words tactlessly uttered before a woman who was leaving the house that had been her home for more years than she probably cared to remember and he was suddenly irritated by his cousin.

Harriet said swiftly: 'You've known the house for some time then?'

'All my life . . . I was born in the

Vicarage across the road,' David told her, smiling. 'I left the village when I was still a child but I've always wanted to come back.'

'I see,' she said slowly, faintly dismayed by the quick thought that he had combined with his detestable cousin in the task of talking a confused old lady into parting with her home for a mere pittance. She was disappointed for she had been inclined to like him and to think well of him . . .

Andrew said briskly: 'Well, Miss Burns . . . I expect you are anxious to complete the formalities and be on your way. Shall we go in?' He allowed her to lead the way into the house but brushed past her in the hall to throw open the door of a large and over-furnished room. 'Just look at this rosewood cabinet, David,' he exclaimed with all the enthusiasm of an antique lover. 'It really is a gem!'

David paused by the door, a faint frown in his eyes while Andrew enthused about the cabinet and then turned his attention to a small table. He turned to smile at Harriet Burns in a kind of apology for his tactless cousin . . . and met her clear, thoughtful gaze. He felt an odd little shock — the sudden, unexpected impact of her personality.

'Do you care about antiques, Mr Mellish?' Harriet asked politely.

His smile deepened, warming his eyes. 'Not as much as I should, I'm afraid,' he said softly, almost conspiratorially. 'My cousin is the expert, of course.'

'Of course,' she agreed impulsively, dryly — and they looked at each other and laughed in warm and friendly understanding. Andrew had discovered anew the perfect proportions and exquisite carving of an old chair and did not hear the exchange of remarks or notice their amusement at his expense.

Harriet coloured slightly as she realized the evident admiration in the very blue eyes that briefly held her own. She looked away in slight confusion — and turned thankfully to the door as the sudden squeal of brakes announced that Rae had finally arrived in her fast sports car.

Rae Carpenter had a great deal of vivacious charm to compensate for lack of beauty. She was small and slight with enormous dark eyes, lively and very intelligent, that dominated the rather plain face and redeemed it from ugliness. The dark, silky hair was cut by an expert and clung to the small head like a cap and she wore the clothes she designed and made for herself with a decided flair. She designed clothes for a living, very successfully . . . and was clever enough to design for just a few, very special people. An actress with an unusual beauty that needed an unusual setting; a singer of popular songs who enjoyed wearing some of Rae's more outrageous designs; a famous novelist who was seen here, there and everywhere; a wealthy young socialite who was always in the news; a Member of Parliament whose elegance was a byword in the House; a minor royal. A mere handful of women who went to Rae Carpenter because she knew exactly the kind of clothes they liked to wear . . . and because she designed exclusively for them.

She had been Harriet's closest friend at the private school in Cashing that they both attended and it was characteristic of Rae that she had kept in touch during the years since their schooldays despite the vast difference in their life-styles. Her circle of friends had become so wide that she might have been forgiven for forgetting all about Harriet. But it was exactly like her to write that warm and friendly letter as soon as she heard about Aunt Sarah's death . . . just as it was like her to insist on driving down to collect Harriet and her luggage.

Rae kissed her warmly and then stood back, surveying her with a critical eye. Then she nodded. 'Certainly an improvement, darling,' she said lightly. 'The suit may not be a Carpenter original but it is presentable. You have taste, Harriet!'

'Thank heavens you approve! I've been terrified that you'd groan at the sight of it — and it cost rather more than I meant to pay. I couldn't afford not to wear it,' Harriet exclaimed, laughing.

'It was worth every penny,' Rae told her lightly. 'You look very elegant. Now, what's happening? Are you ready to leave? My Mama has laid on a splendid luncheon and invited some of her cronies so you are being launched into society with a vengeance, I'm afraid.'

'Oh no!' Harriet exclaimed in dismay.

'I know,' Rae commiserated. 'But we'll escape at the earliest possible moment . . . I'll remember an urgent appointment.'

Harriet linked her hand in her friend's arm and drew her towards the house. 'Come on in,' she said warmly. 'I only have to hand over the keys and sign some papers. But

I'm glad you're here . . . I can use a little moral support.'

Rae was not listening. She was looking at the man who was framed in the open doorway of the house . . . and her eyes had narrowed ominously. She halted and said brusquely; 'I won't come in . . . I'll wait for you in the car.'

Startled, Harriet began a protest . . . but she was interrupted by Andrew Preston who strode down the path towards them. 'Rae . . . ' he exclaimed, his voice sounding slightly strangled. 'What are you doing here?'

With a tilt to her chin, Rae faced him. 'I might ask you the same question,' she returned and her tone dripped with ice. 'I can assure you that I had no idea you'd be here or wild horses wouldn't have dragged me within ten miles of this place!'

He flushed and glanced at Harriet in obvious discomfiture. Anger and embarrassment struggled for supremacy in his expression. 'Please try to be adult, Rae,' he said stiffly. 'I didn't contrive this, you know ... I was not even aware that you knew Miss Burns.'

'Oh, Harriet and I are old friends,' she returned coolly. 'Most of my friends do remain loyal to me despite the life I lead, you see!'

The shaft went home and he stiffened. 'If you mean to drag up ancient quarrels then there is no point in talking to you,' he said angrily.

'I've no wish to listen to anything you have to say, anyway,' she said bluntly. 'I washed you out of my hair a long time ago, Andrew.'

Harriet hovered in an agony of embarrassment, feeling she should leave them to enjoy their quarrel and yet feeling she ought to intervene before either or both said something to be regretted. She looked towards the house and saw that David Mellish stood in the porch, watching the angry couple with a faintly rueful amusement in his eyes.

She walked towards him, her going

scarcely noticed by the couple who were still glaring at each other in angry silence. 'What shall I do?' she asked anxiously, an unconscious appeal in her eyes as she reached David Mellish.

He smiled. 'Leave them to it,' he said lightly. 'They are always the same . . . cat and dog isn't in it! Perhaps you would care to go over the house with me while they fight it out?'

She nodded and led the way into the house. 'I didn't know they knew each other,' she said wryly. 'I feel quite guilty about bringing them together!'

'Don't worry about it,' David said reassuringly. 'They are always running into each other — and not always by accident. I sometimes think they enjoy hurting each other! They were engaged at one time, you know.'

Harriet shook her head. 'I didn't know. Oh, I remember that Rae was engaged to someone before she went to live in London but I never knew the man's name and it was all over so quickly. I never knew why it ended.'

'They quarrelled because Rae wanted to go to London and Andrew wanted to get married. He wanted a wife who would sit at home and bring up the children — and Rae knew she had a talent that ought not to be wasted. Andrew thought she would come running home with her tail between her legs within a few weeks and he can't forgive her for being such a success. And Rae can't forgive him for thinking so little of her flair for design. It's an explosive relationship . . . and the pity of it is that they still care for each other.'

Harriet glanced at him swiftly, incredulously, the angry words still echoing in her ears. 'Do they?' she asked dryly.

David laughed. 'I know it seems unlikely,' he admitted. 'But there's never been any other woman for Andrew . . . and for all the men in Rae's life there never seems to be anyone special, does there?'

'I've no idea,' Harriet said frankly.

'I knew Rae at school and we've kept more or less in touch ever since but I know very little about her life in recent years. We've moved along very different paths since our schooldays.'

David fancied there was a faint trace of bitterness behind the words. He was silent for a moment. Then he said quietly: 'May I ask what you mean to do now, Miss Burns? Forgive me . . . but I gather that you've been looking after your aunt and haven't had much chance to lead your own life. I daresay you mean to spread your wings and enjoy your freedom. But I can't help feeling that I've turned you out into the snow, so to speak. If there is anything I can do . . . anything at all . . . ?'

Harriet said quickly: 'Thank you . . . you are very kind. But I shall be all right. I am going to stay with Rae for a few days. I shall soon get a job and a flat of my own . . . you really needn't feel the slightest concern for me, Mr Mellish.'

He bent his head to look at her faintly flushed face, a smile in his blue eyes. 'Are you offended?' he asked gently. 'I didn't mean to imply that you aren't perfectly capable of looking after yourself, you know.'

The colour deepend in her face. 'It's all right. I didn't mean to be rude . . . I'm sorry. But I don't want anyone to feel responsible for me . . . not in any way! Can you understand? I want to be my own mistress and take care of myself!'

David believed that he did understand. She was obviously very proud and very jealous of her newfound independence. Without knowing the facts, he suspected that she had always been dependent on her great-aunt for everything and forced to swallow her pride throughout the years . . . it would be very natural for her to want to show the world that she was quite capable of standing on her own feet. He was suddenly aware that his interest in Harriet Burns was not to be easily dismissed. He wanted very much to know how she was going to cope with a world that she obviously knew very little about. He wanted very much to be at hand if she needed help or advice at any time. He wanted very much to know her better and to be her friend . . .

'Will I see you again?' he said abruptly, surprising himself by uttering the words that were in his mind.

About to take him though to the kitchen Harriet paused with her hand on the doorknob and turned to look at him in surprise. 'I don't know,' she said slowly. 'I may never come back to Calderwick.'

'I'm expressing myself badly,' David said ruefully, smiling at her. 'I meant . . . may I see you in town? Take you out to dinner one evening, perhaps?'

Meeting his eyes, Harriet felt a shaft of delight. It was the first time in six years that she had seen warm admiration in a man's eyes . . . and this was a handsome, personable man of the world who found her attractive and wanted to take her out! She told herself that it was amazing what a new suit and a change of lipstick could do for a girl . . . and a little smile lurked in her grey eyes at the thought.

'I should like that,' she said simply and without hesitation.

David nodded. He approved her candour and her directness. So many women were unnecessarily coy at such moments. He liked Harriet Burns and did not hesitate to let her know it and there was absolutely no reason why she should hesitate to admit that she liked him in return. She did — or she would not have agreed to meet him in town so readily. 'Then we'll make it a definite date, shall we?' he said confidently. 'Monday next? Seven o'clock? I'll pick you up at Rae's flat.'

Harriet blinked slightly. She was not used to such swift and decisive arrangements. 'I expect that will be all right,' she said, a little doubtfully.

David took out his wallet and extracted one of his cards and handed it to her. 'That's the address and telephone number of my flat in town,' he said. 'I shall be there all the weekend. If you change your mind or if anything crops up to make Monday difficult for you, all you have to do is telephone. All right?'

Nodding, Harriet tucked the card into her suit pocket . . . and turned swiftly as Andrew Preston strode into the house, his eyes dark with anger and his nostrils flaring slightly. He was breathing hard. Harriet looked at him with a dislike she made no effort to conceal and said involuntarily: 'What's happened to Rae?'

'She said she needed a drink . . . she wants you to join her in the pub when you're ready to go,' he said curtly. 'I gather you are expected for lunch in Cashing so I mustn't keep you any longer, Miss Burns.' He drew a sheaf of papers from the briefcase that lay on the hall table and laid them out in order for her signature. The formalities were soon completed and Harriet tucked her handbag under her arm and stooped to pick up her cases. She was swiftly forestalled by David Mellish.

'Let me take those,' he said in a tone that brooked no argument. He smiled down at her. 'Is there any reason why I shouldn't buy you and Rae a drink before you dash away?'

Harriet laughed, suddenly light-hearted and a little light-headed with a sense of freedom. 'I can't think of any objection,' she said gaily.

He turned to his cousin. 'And you, Andrew . . . I insist! This is a big day for Calderwick, you know! The return of the prodigal!'

'I'm all right,' Andrew said, a little sharply. 'Go ahead . . . I'll hang around here.'

'Don't be an idiot!' David told him bluntly. 'You know damn well that you're itching to make it up with Rae . . . and I should think the sight of a woman crying into her beer would melt the hardest heart!'

A reluctant smile tugged at Andrew's lips. 'If we find Rae crying into her beer then I'll pay for the drinks!' he said grimly, seized one of Harriet's cases from his cousin's hand and marched off down the path.

David winked at Harriet. 'One has to make allowances,' he said lightly. 'He's been impossible ever since he was crossed in love — but his heart's in the right place.'

A gurgle of laughter escaped her and he smiled at her with swift approval. As they walked towards the gate together, he took her arm with a casual friendliness, a hint of intimacy, a slight air of protective interest . . . and Harriet was alarmed by a sudden little surge of response to his obvious liking and admiration. Instinctively she drew herself a little away and it was almost a rebuff. She scarcely knew David Mellish and she must not allow herself to be carried away on the strength of one meeting, she told herself firmly. He was a man of the world and his attentions probably meant very little. It might be very flattering that he admired her and made no secret of it . . . at the same time, she was not such an innocent as he might suppose and she had no intention of being swept off her feet by a good-looking man who might well be a determined womaniser for all she knew. It would be foolish to rush into liking him just because he had very blue eyes that crinkled endearingly when he smiled . . .

Harriet's cases were stowed in the back of Rae's sleek and shining sports car and then the trio crossed the road to join her in the pub. Rae was at the bar, chatting to the landlord as though he was an old friend. Andrew went to her and put an arm about her thin shoulders and bent down to murmur something into her ear. Rae looked up, smiled, pulled his head down to kiss him briefly on the lips . . . and continued her conversation with the landlord as though nothing had happened.

Harriet stared . . . and David smiled a little wryly, noting her expression. It was very obvious that she was a newcomer to Rae's world and way of life and he wondered what she would make of it all when she was staying with Rae who was a law unto herself and quite unpredictable at times and cultivated some very odd friends . . .

Harriet stared . . . and her heart twisted in sudden envy. So that was loving when angry, hurtful words were forgotten in a moment and forgiven with a kiss. Andrew stood beside Rae, her hand held tightly within his own, his gaze warm and tender as he looked down at her — and there was intense, unquestioning love in every line of his body.

Harriet suddenly ached for the kind of loving that they so obviously knew for each other . . . and she knew with desperate intensity that she wanted little from life but to love and be loved. Given the right opportunities she would follow every rainbow until she found her dream . . . the kind of loving that brought lasting happiness and rich fulfilment to her life.

David spoke to her twice before she seemed to be aware of his voice . . . and he wondered what had been in her mind, what thoughts had brought that soft, misty wistfulness to the grey eyes and a sweetness to the mouth that he abruptly ached to kiss. But the desire held tenderness rather than passion . . . and he was shaken to realize the impact of this woman on his heart and mind in so short a time.

She turned to him with dreams still in her eyes and in her smile . . . and in that moment David knew that she was the one woman he had waited all his life to love with his entire being. He had supposed himself in love before . . . but it had never been like this. Such a wealth of conviction. Such an intensity of knowing. Such a sureness that it was for real and for ever.

Their eyes met and held and emotion welled in him and he knew that he loved this enchanting stranger and he smiled down at her with love and spoke . . .

'What will you have . . . lager, sherry, gin and something?'

He wanted to offer her the moon, the stars, his heart, his entire life . . . but it was much too soon and he believed he had already alarmed her a little with his impatience to begin the intimacy of friendship . . .

4

The silver sports car ate up the miles as it sped down the wide road towards the metropolis, rather later in the day than anticipated.

They had been late for the splendid luncheon arranged by Rae's mother and it had been impossible to rush away immediately after the meal. Rae's foot was hard on the accelerator for she was going to a party that evening.

Harriet was silent, a little subdued now that the long-awaited escape from the narrow confines of Calderwick had been finally achieved. It was one thing to long desperately for one's freedom . . . quite another to have it within one's grasp and not really know what to do with it. Habit was soul destroying, she thought wryly. Each day had been so much like the one before for so long that now a very different way of life was spread out before her she scarcely knew whether to be glad or sorry. In fact, she was just a little frightened of the great big world that was rushing to meet her . . . and very thankful that she had Rae to help her over the first hurdles.

'How do you feel?' Rae asked suddenly, as though she had caught the thought.

Harriet grimaced. 'Sick . . . ' she said lightly.

'Just nerves,' Rae said reassuringly. 'But you've nothing to worry about . . . I'll keep you under my wing for a while. You'll be all right. It'll be fun, you'll see.'

'I'm so stupidly shy,' Harriet said wryly. 'I dread meeting people for the first time . . . I never know what to say to them! I usually say far too much — and all the wrong things!'

'Oh nonsense! You were perfectly cool and composed at lunch — and meeting my Mama's friends is an ordeal for anyone!'

'I was shaking inside!'

Rae laughed. 'That doesn't matter . . . it didn't show! I admire your ability to seem so cool, calm and collected . . . it's a great asset, Harriet!'

'Aunt Sarah didn't encourage me to show my feelings very much,' Harriet said quietly.

'Good for Aunt Sarah! There's nothing more embarrassing for others than a display of emotions. Which reminds me . . . I owe you an apology, Harriet. I could have used a little of Aunt Sarah's discipline myself, I guess. But I didn't expect to come face to face with Andrew like that and it was a shock . . . I haven't seen him in months. But that doesn't excuse the fact that you had to witness a childish and very silly squabble.'

'Oh, don't worry . . . it all blew over, anyway,' Harriet said, a little uncertainly. 'I just wish I'd known . . . I mean, it could have been avoided — it must have been painful for you both . . . '

'I was pleased to see him,' Rae said

quietly. 'So damn pleased that I was furious with myself . . . that's why I flew at him! I thought I was over him . . . I've tried hard enough to stop wanting him, heaven knows!' She laughed ruefully. 'This love business is the very devil, Harriet — be warned! It isn't a bit like the books lead you to think, you know . . . love and laughter and happy ever after! What do they call it — romantic fiction? How apt? Believe me, there's nothing romantic about love . . . it's a painful, miserable, demanding, degrading experience and the most you can hope for is the kitchen sink and the baby's nappies at the end of it! But I suppose the young have to be brainwashed into believing that boy plus girl plus sex equals eternal happiness or the entire structure of our society might collapse!'

Harriet was faintly shocked. But a moment's thought satisfied her that the words could only be born of Rae's desperate longing for the kitchen sink and the baby's nappies and life as the wife of the man she still loved despite the ending of their engagement. Her heart went out to her unhappy friend even while she marvelled that two people could be so foolish as to allow pride to stand in the way of their happiness. When one loved, surely pride simply did not exist, she thought in all innocence . . .

She said lightly: 'Thanks for the warning . . . I'll keep it in mind. But my chances of falling in love seem rather remote . . . I don't know any likely men!'

'You will!' Rae prophesied confidently. Without conscious connection although she had observed the man's interest and admiration for her friend, she went on lightly: 'Isn't it incredible how things work out . . . that it should have been David Mellish who bought your aunt's house? He's never mentioned it . . . not that there was the slightest reason why he should, of course. We know each other but not that well. His mother is one of my clients and David and I meet occasionally at parties and things. I wonder what you'll make of Polly — I think she's a fantastic person! Do you know her books? The earlier ones caused a sensation in their day!'

'Do you mean Polly Prior?' Harriet asked. 'Aunt Sarah adored her books. Do you mean that she's David Mellish's mother?'

'Of course!' Rae glanced at her in surprise. 'Did you really not know? Has he never mentioned it?'

'We only met for the first time today.'

'How odd! I thought you were old friends!'

Harriet smiled, remembering the warm glow of pleasure she had known when she first realized that he admired her as an attractive and personable woman.

They hit heavy traffic as they reached the suburbs of the city and Rae needed to concentrate on the road. Harriet admired her friend's skill as the car wove in and out of the traffic. She marvelled that Rae could cope so well with the alarming and enormous transcontinental lorries that seemed to dominate the road. Rae drove well, braking, accelerating, changing gear, slipping from one lane to another with the ease of experience. Soon they were close to the hub of the city and Harriet was too eager to look about her to worry about the traffic congestion.

Hyde Park Corner brought them to a complete standstill and Rae explained that it was rush hour traffic that she had hoped to avoid by leaving early . . . they were trapped between two buses with a sea of cars and taxis on all sides and no apparent way out of the impasse. But the arrival of a policeman on a motor-cycle soon brought order out of confusion . . . and a very few minutes later, Rae brought the car to a halt outside a tall block of luxury flats that overlooked the park.

Harriet was surprised by the size and splendour of her friend's home and delighted to discover that the windows provided a marvellous view of Hyde Park and the Serpentine. Situated on the eighth floor, high above the traffic, the flat was quiet and peaceful and very comfortable. There was a service restaurant which Rae admitted to using far more than the small, well-fitted kitchen . . . she was not a domesticated animal, she confessed carelessly.

Harriet had her own bedroom and she was touched to discover that Rae had provided a bowl of roses to welcome her. 'Now this is really spoiling me!' she exclaimed warmly.

Rae laughed. 'Why not? We're all entitled to a little spoiling at times . . . and heaven knows you've earned it! Looking after the gargoyle all these years hasn't been much fun for you, I know!'

'Poor Aunt Sarah!' Harriet said slowly. 'She had such an empty, meaningless life . . . and never wanted it any other way. How can anyone be satisfied with so little from life?'

'She didn't give much so she didn't

get much,' Rae said bluntly. 'Don't waste your sympathy, Harriet. From now on you must think about yourself and no one else! Aunt Sarah wanted your life to be as empty and meaningless as hers — and you must see to it that it isn't! I've found you a job, by the way.'

Harriet looked up from the suitcase she had begun to unpack. 'You have . . . What is it?'

'I have a friend who owns a boutique in Knightsbridge. One of her girls has gone off to Canada at a moment's notice and I told Clare that you'd fill in until you find something you really want to do. How do you feel about it?'

Harriet felt doubtful and looked it. 'I know nothing about fashion?'

'You'll soon learn,' Rae said confidently. 'Clare will break you in gently and it's something you can do — and I know you'll enjoy it.'

'I haven't any qualifications for any kind of job,' Harriet said ruefully.

'Except as a nurse companion for old ladies!'

'That's out!' Rae exclaimed firmly. 'I'm in charge of your life now . . . and old ladies definitely have no part in it!'

Harriet smiled but she felt troubled. She was grateful to Rae, of course . . . more than grateful. But she had wanted to be done with gratitude. She had wanted to stand on her own feet at last. She had wanted to find her own job and discover that she could look after herself and her interests. Rae was a dear, a good friend . . . but the hint of dominance in her manner was almost more than she could bear.

Rae was swift to notice the shadow that crossed her face. She said quickly: 'I'm only joking, you know. I don't really mean to run your life. I should think you've had more than enough of that kind of thing — and I should be hopeless at it, anyway. I can't run my own life very successfully,' she added untruthfully. 'If you don't care for the idea of working for Clare just say so . . . no harm done!'

Harriet responded readily to the swift understanding and the warm reassurance . . . and knew she was fortunate in Rae's friendship. 'I know I can opt out if I wish, Rae . . . but I don't wish. Working in a boutique will be fun — totally different to Calderwick and that's what I want! I'm grateful, really.'

'Look, no gratitude!' Rae disclaimed swiftly. 'You're doing Clare the favour! She needs someone quickly and the right kind of girl is hard to find. I think you're just right — and so will she! I merely happened to be in the position to know about the job and to tell you that it's yours if you want it . . . no effort on my part at all! Don't thank me until you've tried it — you might hate the boutique!'

Harriet's eyes twinkled. 'Dare I mention how grateful I am that you've provided me with a roof over my head until I can find a flat . . . or will you jump down my throat again?'

Rae laughed. 'I suppose I could tell you that the flat is much too big and I rattle about in it like a solitary pea in an enormous pod. Actually, the flat is just right and I'm too scatter-brained for anyone to put up with me for long. But you're very welcome to stay as long as you want — and I shall love having you.' She glanced at her watch. 'I must change into my party gear. Are you sure you won't come, Harriet? You have to start meeting people soon, you know.'

'I'm rather tired,' Harriet said truthfully.

It had been an emotionally exhausting day and she would be glad to relax and she did not mind being left on her own while Rae went off to her party. In fact, she was glad that Rae's unerring instinct had led her to go ahead with her plans for the evening although it was Harriet's first few hours away from Calderwick and the old life. She knew that Harriet did not want her or anyone else hovering over her, worrying about her, feeling responsible for her . . . she wanted to be perfectly free to get on with living her own life in her own way.

So Rae went off to her party in a striking flame-coloured dress . . . and Harriet finished unpacking and tidied her bedroom and changed from her fashionable suit to old slacks and a shabby, shapeless but very comfortable sweater. She felt very much at home in the flat and it surprised her a little that she had adapted so readily to new surroundings and felt scarcely the slightest excitement at the knowledge that a gay, glittering and very glamorous city was all about her in the place of the sleepy little village.

She pottered about the little kitchen, making herself a snack which was all she wanted after the heavy meal in the middle of the day. She watched television with all the wide-eyed wonder of a newcomer to its marvels . . . but soon switched it off, feeling too restless to settle in the deep armchair. She wondered if she dared to go for a walk if only to explore the famous park . . . even losing herself would be adventurous after all the uneventful years. While she hesitated, no longer weary and very much disinclined to go meekly to bed on her first night in London, the doorbell pealed.

She opened the door to a tall man who was just about to press the bell once more. Harriet felt the swift impact of his very good looks as he smiled in casual greeting. 'Hallo, sweetie,' he said lightly and walked past her with a supreme confidence. She left it just a little too late to protest . . . and it would have been difficult to refuse admission to a man so obviously determined to enter, so obviously at home in the flat, so obviously one of Rae's more intimate friends. Yet she felt uneasy, her heart jumping a little with faint apprehension for he was a stranger and she was alone with him in this quiet flat in the heart of a suddenly alarming city.

He looked round the empty sitting-room, glanced through the open door of Rae's bedroom and turned to the young woman who watched him, her eyes narrowed in faint suspicion. He smiled at her reassuringly. 'Rae is out, I guess?'

'I'm afraid so . . . she's gone to a party,' Harriet said, a little stiffly.

'Duncan's party?'

'I really don't know . . . I don't think she said,' Harriet replied uncertainly.

'That sounds like Rae,' he said carelessly. 'Well, I'm not chasing all over London to find her . . . not tonight, anyway.' He sank into an armchair and took out his cigarette case.

Harriet perched on the arm of the sofa, not very happy about the situation and wondering if she would often be called upon to entertain Rae's friends in her absence. He drew deeply on his cigarette and exhaled the blue smoke with a faint sigh. Relaxing, he leaned back in the chair and closed his eyes ... and Harriet, studying him, thought that he looked tired and a little drawn and oddly vulnerable. Like a handsome little boy, she thought foolishly ... and soft colour stole into her face as he opened his eyes and caught her watching him.

Meeting the clear and very lovely eyes, he smiled ... the slow, endearing smile that had bewitched many a woman — and Harriet's heart jumped once more but not with apprehension. She responded quite instinctively to the warm, fascinating charm of that smile — and was suddenly femininely conscious of her shabby sweater and tousled hair.

'No party for you, Cinderella?' he asked lightly, a little curiously, aware that she reacted to him as did most women and beginning to wonder about her.

'I didn't want to go ... '

He nodded with understanding. 'I don't blame you ... some of these parties are very boring affairs. Too many people, too much noise! A quiet dinner for two is much more to my taste. How about you?'

'I haven't been to many parties,' Harriet returned simply.

He wondered if the suggestion in his words had totally escaped her or if she merely chose to ignore it. His glance dwelt on her, a little lingeringly . . . and as her chin tilted just a fraction with swift resentment he felt his interest quicken.

'We haven't met before, have we?' he said lightly. 'I never forget a face — and yours is particularly memorable. I'm Warren Hailey . . . perhaps Rae has mentioned me occasionally?' He smiled, his eyes twinkling at the mocking self-deprecation of his words . . . as if she could fail to recognize that very famous name!

Harriet shook her head. 'I don't think so.' She smiled with faint apology. 'I know very little about Rae's friends and I haven't had much chance to meet any of them yet. I only arrived in town today.'

Warren was slightly shattered. But a glance convinced him that his name really had not made any impression . . . she was not just slapping him down. He wondered where she could have spent the last few years! Those candid eyes, meeting his so honestly, assured him that she could not dissemble or deceive and again he felt that spark of interest. For this was a very different kind of woman — and how bored he was with the women in his life!

'An oversight, obviously,' he said lightly. 'Rae and I are old friends . . . I'm sure she *must* mention me one day.' He was delighted to notice the faint tugging of a smile at her lovely mouth. 'In the meantime, I shall just have to recommend myself to you — which I do, very highly.'

Harriet chuckled. 'Naturally.'

He warmed to her even more and his smile conveyed the fact. 'By the way, do you have a name — or do you prefer to answer to Cinderella?'

'I'm Harriet Burns,' she told him readily.

'*Miss* Harriet Burns?'

Her grey eyes danced suddenly. 'Oh, yes.'

'Good! Now we can really get to know each other,' he said lightly. 'We'll have a party of our own, shall we? I know a very nice restaurant where we can wine, dine and even dance a little.' He leaned forward abruptly and compelled her gaze with the sheer force of his personality — and Harriet's heart began to race with excitement. 'I want to know you, Harriet Burns . . . very much indeed,' he said softly.

Suddenly all her resistance melted . . . for he was very attractive and she could not help liking him and being amused by his audacious charm. She reminded herself that she had been determined on a very different way of life . . . and what could be more different than accepting this unexpected, exciting invitation from a handsome stranger to experience her first taste of London night-life?

She smiled at him, a little shyly, very sweetly. 'I'd love to come to your party,' she said, throwing all caution to the four winds . . .

5

From a quiet backwater, Harriet was flung into the whirlpool of life as Warren Hailey's new girl-friend . . . and she soon discovered that her ignorance of his fame and brilliance as a society photographer had betrayed the unusual background to her life. For Warren's name was internationally known and it was only to quiet villages such as Calderwick that his fame had not yet penetrated.

Harriet scarcely had time to draw a deep breath during those first few days. It would have been more than enough for any girl in her particular circumstances to begin life and work in London with all its sophistication and glamour without the added excitement of attracting someone like Warren Hailey.

He was attracted and very attentive.

He was also reputed to be extremely selective in his choice of women-friends. It was said that he demanded beauty and intelligence and character in a woman . . . and so Harriet was acclaimed as a beautiful, intelligent and very exciting newcomer. She was amused for she was shrewd enough to appreciate that Warren's interest ensured her place in his circle of friends and that without him to sponsor her she might not have excited the slightest ripple of attention. She knew that she was not beautiful or particularly clever and far from exciting and she was unmoved by most of the flattering admiration that came her way. She received far more invitations than she could possibly accept — and meant to enjoy herself for as long as Warren's interest should last. She knew it could not last long . . . she was merely someone new, someone different. She was inexperienced but she was not a fool and she realized that there had been many women in Warren's life and that he had been spoiled by their eager response to his attentions.

But she was sure that he was sincere in his liking and admiration for her . . . and that was very satisfying to a long-suppressed feminine ego. She liked him very much and enjoyed his company and responded eagerly if a little shyly to the ardour in his pursuit — but she had no intention of losing her head. He had a great deal of charm and a very persuasive manner and she had swiftly become fond of him but she did not mean to join the ranks of his past mistresses.

Warren thought her delightful and intriguing and tantalising. She was an odd mixture of passion and prudery, he discovered . . . a sensual, seductive little witch in his arms one moment and an evasive, distant and quite determined virgin the next! He never quite knew when a word or a caress or a gesture would send her scuttling for safety with a look in her lovely eyes that made him feel like an absolute heel . . . never knew just how far she would allow him to go before she slammed the door in his face. He wanted her more than he had ever wanted any woman . . . and all the more because he had an infuriating suspicion that he would never own her! She was not the least in love with him, he realized . . . and that was a new experience in itself for Warren Hailey, who had known women to fall in love with him at the drop of a hat!

There was a great deal more to Harriet than her elusiveness as a conquest, of course. He delighted in her swift appreciation of all that she had never seen or experienced before and it gave him real pleasure to show her the London he knew so intimately. They did the sights like a couple of tourists . . . and she was an eager, sparkling child in her breathless delight and spontaneous response to the sights and sounds of the city. She could be grave and thoughtful one moment, gay and sparkling the next . . . shy and reserved and distant one moment, suddenly confident and warmly responsive and totally enchanting the next. He had never known a woman quite like her and could not quite pin down the quality of her appeal. But the tall, slender girl with the pale hair and wide grey eyes and the odd ability to convey a beauty she did not possess already meant a great deal to him . . . and it did not even occur to him to slow the pace despite his long-held conviction that he was not cut out for a lasting relationship with any woman . . .

It was a whirlwind weekend and one that Harriet would never forget . . . Warren had proved to be a wonderful, exciting companion in this new and wonderful and exciting world!

But when Monday dawned, she came down to earth and went off to the boutique with the determination to erase any lingering memories of the silly mistakes she had made on the previous Friday, her very first day as a working girl.

Clare was delighted with her new assistant and had expected her to make a few mistakes until she found her feet. She had been a little dubious about the whole business but Rae had been very persuasive and the very first moment of meeting Harriet Burns had told the shrewd business-woman that she would be a valuable asset. She was tall and she had an excellent figure and an old-fashioned quality called grace that so many girls of her generation seemed to lack. She moved well and easily and she possessed an air of quiet elegance that pleased Clare who counted some members of very high society among her clients. She soon discovered that Harriet Burns was also totally frank. In her anxiety to make a sale she would not foist a totally unsuitable garment on a hesitating client with a little flattering patter . . . she told the truth even at the risk of offending and took pains to find just the right thing. And she was so obviously genuine in her concern and interest and had such a feeling for style and suitability and a remarkable instinct for handling people that Clare was very willing to forgive the loss of the few clients who disliked and resented the girl's honesty. The satisfied ones would return and bring their friends . . . and that was the really important thing.

It was a very busy day, much busier than usual thanks to society's curiosity about the newcomer to their ranks and the ripple of information along the grapevine that she was to be found at Clare's of Knightsbridge. Harriet, innocent of the ways of this new world, was merely pleased and a little flattered to be recognized and warmly greeted by a number of women she had met over the weekend while escorted by Warren to various functions and places. She coped with curious questions as best she could and made no secret of the quiet and uneventful life she had led before coming to London. The light and not so subtle innuendoes about her relationship with Warren were disconcerting but she accepted their inevitability . . . he was a well-known personality and he had not attempted to conceal his reputation where women were concerned. She was quite willing to admit the newness of her friendship with him and the fact that they had met through his friendship with Rae . . . and it was only then that she wondered, as she had perhaps been intended to wonder, why Rae had been so oddly reticent during the last few days. Harriet assumed that it was a tactful avoidance of interference or giving unwanted advice . . . but perhaps Rae was too hurt or too angry or too jealous to care for her sudden association with Warren Hailey.

Halfway through the afternoon, out of the blue, came the recollection of her promise to dine with David Mellish that evening. She had double-dated herself! For Warren planned to take her to a new nightclub on the river near Richmond and she was looking forward to it. She recalled that David Mellish had provided her with an escape clause if she should need it but she could not remember what she had done with his card. Of course it must be a simple matter to find out his telephone number . . . Rae would probably know it. But what excuse could she give him for not keeping the appointment. She could not lie to him.

She told herself sternly that she had been very glad to accept his invitation when it was offered and it was just unfortunate that she had since met Warren who wanted to monopolize her free time. She could not wriggle out of her date with David Mellish at the last moment. She would just have to explain the circumstances to Warren and arrange to go out with him the following evening.

Warren was not at all pleased but there was nothing he could say to make her change her mind . . . and he had to admit the justice of her argument and admire her integrity. There was some compensation in the fact that she had completely forgotten the appointment . . . and even more consolation in the fact that David's approach to women was even more unemotional than his own and he need not fear him as a serious rival . . .

Rae wandered into the bedroom while Harriet was getting ready to go out that evening. She noted the sophisticated gown that lay across the bed, the fashionable evening sandals and the matching evening bag. She regarded her friend with mixed feelings. She was delighted that Harriet was beginning to live at last and to enjoy the feminine luxuries and pleasures that she had been denied until now . . . but she could not help wishing that she had chosen a very different man to introduce her to London life and society.

Rae was fond of Warren and included him among her friends but she had no illusions about him. They had met when Thelma McCall, the actress, had commissioned him to photograph her in the beautiful outfits that Rae had designed for a new play . . . and immediate attraction had leaped between them. They had enjoyed a brief, superficial and wholly delightful affair that neither regretted. But it was one thing for Rae to plunge into a reckless and rapturous affair with a man like Warren Hailey, knowing exactly what she was doing and how it would end — quite another for an innocent like Harriet to become involved with him. No doubt her very innocence constituted her greatest appeal — and it would probably never occur to Warren that she was the intense type to fall deeply in love and suffer by his eventual and inevitable wearying. Warren might not appreciate that her innocence was exactly that and she was terribly vulnerable because of it. Harriet was an absolute child in these matters and had such a touching faith in human nature that she probably assumed that Warren's determined pursuit meant

that he was desperate to marry her
. . . and Rae knew without a shadow of
doubt that love and marriage played no
part at all in Warren's lifestyle . . .

But she had said nothing to disillusion
Harriet or to discourage her from seeing
so much of Warren. She knew that her
friend was still reacting from the long
years of suppression and that the least
hint of opposition to her friendship with
Warren would merely drive her further
into his arms . . .

'Meeting Warren . . . ?' she asked
lightly and with casual interest.

Harriet shook her head. 'David
Mellish,' she said. 'He's taking me
out to dinner . . . calling for me at
seven. It's nearly that now, isn't it?'

'Ten to seven. You really have taken
London by storm, haven't you?' she
teased gently, watching as Harriet
carefully outlined her lovely mouth.
She had proved to be a quick learner
and she already knew all the latest
trends in hair and make-up and clothes.
But she knew what suited her and she

was wise enough not to follow fashion too closely. 'What happened to the shy little mouse who jumped if a man so much as spoke to her?'

Harriet laughed. 'I don't think I was ever quite that bad,' she demurred, reaching for the black velvet dress and stepping into it. She turned her back towards Rae who obediently zipped the back of the dress. 'I'd forgotten all about this date with David Mellish,' Harriet admitted frankly. 'He asked me on Thursday and I suppose I leaped at it . . . I didn't know that I was going to meet Warren, after all. I'm afraid he's rather cross about it but I don't think it would have been fair to break the date.'

'One can never have too many friends,' Rae agreed lightly. 'There are always one or two who fall by the wayside.'

Harriet turned to look at her, meeting the dark eyes steadily. 'Are you trying to warn me that Warren is likely to fall by the wayside?' she asked in her direct way.

'It could happen,' Rae said quietly. 'You aren't the first women in his life. I'd like to think that you'll be the last if it means so much to you but I'm afraid it isn't very likely. Does it really matter, Harriet?' she added gently.

Harriet hesitated. 'I don't know,' she said wryly. 'One hears and reads so much about love — but how does one know when it's really loving and not just liking a man very, very much?'

Rae smiled, a hint of tender indulgence in her smile for the naivety of the question. 'When you need to ask then you aren't in love,' she said lightly. 'It's that simple!' The doorbell pealed and she went towards the door. 'That must be David . . . I'll give him a kiss and a drink while you finish titivating.'

Harriet said abruptly: 'Do you mind, Rae — about Warren?'

Rae turned in surprise, an eyebrow raised in faint amusement. 'Mind? Should I?'

'It was you he came to see on Thursday,' Harriet recalled.

'Oh, he frequently calls to see me . . . we like each other,' Rae said carelessly. 'That doesn't make him my property.' She went on, rather brusquely: 'I'll tell you myself before some kindly acquaintance mentions it . . . Warren and I were lovers once. It didn't mean very much . . . it just happened. Now we are friends and that doesn't happen very often. It means more to me that Warren thinks of me as a friend than it ever meant to be involved in that casual affair with him.' The doorbell pealed once more. 'Oh . . . poor David!' she exclaimed and fled.

Suddenly, Harriet was quivering jelly. She was thankful that Rae was there to ease the first awkward moments with a man that she abruptly looked on as a complete stranger. Why, she could not even recall what he looked like, she realized with horror. Thank goodness she had not arranged to meet him elsewhere . . . it would have been too dreadful if she had failed to recognize him or approached the wrong man!

She felt ridiculously nervous and terribly unsure of herself . . . and wished she had not cancelled her evening with Warren. She was so much at ease with Warren who made her laugh and swept her along on the buoyant tide of his own confidence. She surveyed herself critically in the long mirror, wondering if her dress was too plain, too severe, if it was too late to change into something more feminine and more morale-boosting. She tucked a wisp of hair into place, took a deep breath and walked out to greet David Mellish with a bright smile carefully pinned to her lips.

David felt like a callow youth as he rose to his feet, his heart hammering. With a rare clumsiness, he brushed against the low table as he moved towards her. She gave him her hand . . . such a soft, slender and oddly fragile hand, he thought with tenderness — and she was just as lovely as the image he had cherished in his heart and mind for four days. So lovely and yet so distant as she gave him her hand and a cool little smile — and the warm and friendly greeting he had prepared fled from his mind and he said with quiet formality: 'Good evening, Miss Burns.'

'I've kept you waiting . . . I'm sorry,' Harriet said, a trifle breathlessly.

'I believe I am a little early,' he said courteously.

Harriet was foolishly disappointed. She had thought him a very good-looking man but now she realized that he was not so distinctive. But she had spent so much time with Warren, much too handsome for his own good, that any man must suffer by comparison. His eyes really *were* as blue as she remembered, though . . . and if only he would smile, she might discover that he was as attractive as she had believed four days ago. But his manner was very formal and a little off-putting — and she wondered if he was regretting that impulsive invitation and equally impulsive acceptance. Perhaps she should have made some excuse not to meet him, after all . . . ?

She sat beside him in the car, scarcely interested in the plans he outlined for the evening . . . and David, glancing briefly at the still, cool young woman at his side, felt a bitter disappointment. Her indifference was unmistakable although she endeavoured to conceal it with polite responses to his remarks. He did not need to wonder why he was making so little impression for he had not only heard about her friendship with Warren Hailey . . . he had seen them together.

He had been at the bar of a very famous restaurant in Soho when they entered . . . and his heart had turned over at the sight of Harriet, radiant and sparkling for her companion. They were holding hands and laughing at each other, all their awareness only for each other. Neither of them had noticed David — and he had not attempted to attract the attention of his old friend or his new love. He had finished his drink and departed — to walk the dark and echoing streets while he battled with feelings that he had never known before.

Perhaps it was foolish to be so much in love with a woman he had met but once and briefly . . . but it was a deeper and more demanding emotion than any he had ever experienced. He loved Harriet and he longed to cherish and protect and care for her with all his being.

Harriet . . . her very name was magic and yet it died on his lips time after time. or she seemed to be keeping him very firmly at a distance and his heart sank. With any other woman he would have set out to charm her into swift, warm response — and he could be very charming and women usually responded to him with very little hesitation.

But Harriet was not like other women and he was not concerned with light and meaningless flirtation this time. He wanted to marry her . . .

6

Harriet responded dutifully to the light remarks while she shrivelled inwardly with stupid shyness and knew a strangely acute awareness of the man by her side. Stealing the occasional glance at him, she was not reassured by a certain austerity in his expression.

She had the odd conviction that he was keeping her at a distance and she wondered if he already regretted having appeared to encourage her interest. Perhaps he was merely disappointed at second meeting . . . or bored with her company, finding her very different to the articulate and sophisticated women of his world. She told herself wryly that the evening was doomed to disaster and she would probably never see him again. Oddly, considering the constraint she felt and a faint resentment at his attitude, that thought did not give her the slightest satisfaction . . .

David had seats for the first night of a new musical . . . and he was aware that she relaxed in the gay and glittering atmosphere of the famous theatre. For his part, he scarcely knew what was happening on stage . . . all his interest and attention was in Harriet and her swift laughter, her delighted appreciation, her totally absorbed enjoyment of the show.

The magic of her surroundings dispelled some of Harriet's shyness although she was still very much aware that they were strangers. In a moment, she had felt that she had known Warren all her life — but it seemed that she might never know David Mellish any better than she did now.

Constraint returned without rhyme or reason when they left the theatre and went on to the nightclub where he had booked a table. The tension of facing him across the small table, of forcing conversation when they seemed to have so little in common, of pretending enjoyment in the face of apparent indifference, was almost intolerable . . . and Harriet rose thankfully at the suggestion that they should dance.

She loved to dance and her sensual being responded swiftly to music and movement. He was a perfect partner, his steps fitting hers exactly, strength and purpose in his lead . . . and she gave herself up to the unexpected delight of dancing with him.

David held her as close as he dared, his arm about her slender waist, a soft wing of her hair brushing against his cheek. The perfume she wore teased his senses and a nerve began to throb in his jaw. She was lovely, enchanting, wholly desirable — and worlds away because he so obviously did not interest or attract her in the least.

The evening had not been too successful and he did not imagine that she would wish to repeat it. Yet he could not walk out of her life without protest. Loving her did not entitle him to anything, he realized . . . but he wanted and needed her friendship if nothing more. But the complete lack of warm and meaningful communication between them implied that they had met as strangers and would part as strangers!

Moving slowly in his arms to the seductive rhythm of the music, Harriet could not help but be aware of him . . . and she was startled by a sudden impatience that he did not hold her closer to him. She told herself firmly to guard against purely feminine pique because the reserve in his manner implied that he did not find her at all attractive.

She stole a glance at him. He was looking over her head, his expression taut . . . and she felt a little pang of dismay. Perhaps it was stupid but she knew an odd sense of loss as though they had once known each other very well and inexplicably drifted apart. Her hand tightened on his shoulder in unconscious protest . . . and David looked down at her swiftly, releasing her slightly. There was a look in her eyes that he did not understand . . . and it was gone in a moment.

'Do you mind if we sit down?' Harriet said brightly.

'Something wrong . . . ?' he asked with swift concern.

'Aching feet!' she exclaimed lightly. 'I've danced until the small hours every night this weekend!'

He took her back to their table, his hand just brushing her elbow. He replenished her glass with wine and provided her with a cigarette and snapped his lighter into flame . . . attentive but unsmiling.

Harriet had only just begun to smoke and she did not really care for it . . . it was merely one more reaction to Aunt Sarah's dictums of the past. She held the cigarette gingerly between her fingers and took care not to inhale . . . and David, watching her, suddenly smiled.

It was the smile she had anticipated all evening and missed so much . . . the smile that deepened the blue of his eyes and brought swift, attractive warmth to his lean features and confirmed her first instinctive liking for a man who was suddenly human and approachable, after all.

'You look like a naughty little girl with that cigarette,' he told her, amusement and tenderness mingled in his tone.

Harriet laughed. 'I'm defying Aunt Sarah,' she said lightly.

'I know . . . and not enjoying it at all,' he said, his eyes teasing her gently . . . and with just a little more than laughter in their depths.

'True . . . ' she admitted ruefully.

He moved to take the cigarette from her fingers . . . she moved to stub it in the ashtray. And without knowing how it happened, the glowing end of the cigarette was rammed against his hand and he jerked away with an exclamation of pain and shock . . .

'Oh, David!' she exclaimed in dismay. 'I am sorry!' Angry, she stubbed the cigarette until it broke messily in the ashtray. Then she caught his hand to examine it . . . and he allowed her to cradle the smarting fingers while she bent an anxious head over the blistered redness and mourned the accident.

'A very minor disaster,' David said lightly. 'And worth it to discover that you really do know how to say my name!'

She looked up quickly to meet his smiling eyes . . . and swift, warm colour stole into her face. She smiled in rueful response. How stupid to think that he was cold and indifferent when the coldness and indifference had been all on her side, making it impossible for him to establish a warm and reassuring contact. She had been so shy and nervous that she had almost ruined the evening and nearly convinced him that they had nothing in common!

'Well, you've been making me feel like a maiden aunt,' she retorted in laughing self-defence. 'No one but your disapproving cousin ever called me

Miss Burns — and it does something to me!' she added with feeling.

'I'll remember,' David said, smiling . . .

They danced again and this time he held her satisfyingly close, his lips briefly brushing the soft skin of her cheek, the silken wing of her pale hair, the small and shapely lobe of her ear . . . and Harriet trembled, strangely disturbed by feelings that stirred within her . . . a new and delicious kind of excitement leaping to life.

Harriet needed to know that she was an attractive and desirable woman . . . all unconsciously, she was seeking reassurance. Jeremy's default all those years ago had left scars on her heart and mind and the narrowness of life with her great-aunt had almost persuaded her that she was destined for lonely spinsterhood in her turn. At twenty-five, she was almost convinced that she would never inspire deep and lasting love in any man and would never know the fulfilment of all the sweet, aching dreams that lived in every woman's heart. Then, all in a day, she had seen the glow of admiration in the eyes of two men and her heart had lifted with new, unconscious hope.

Sudden freedom had gone to her head a little — and while she had no conscious thought of encouraging either man to love her, she could not help snatching with eager heart and hands at the comforting reassurance in their interest and admiration. So she was thankful to discover that David was not really indifferent to her . . . and she was all woman in her secret delight that Warren had been so transparently jealous of her promise to spend the evening with another man . . .

It was late when David took her home. As the car pulled up outside the block of flats, she stifled a yawn. 'Home with the milk again,' she said, laughing. 'I'm a working girl, too!' She suddenly felt so sleepy that it seemed too much of an effort to get out of the car.

David reached to the back seat for

her wrap and slipped it about her shoulders. For a moment, his hands were stilled and he looked down at her with love in his heart for the sleepy child that she seemed in that long-to-be-cherished moment.

'Goodnight, David,' she said and raised her face to be kissed . . . and sleepiness was abruptly dispelled as she realized how much she wanted him to kiss her.

His hands tightened fiercely, painfully, on her slim shoulders and then she was caught against his hard chest as he held her very close and a button on his jacket bit into her soft breast and she closed her eyes on a wave of fierce, inexplicable longing . . . but he did not kiss her.

David did not trust himself to kiss her. That soft, sensual mouth held the promise of too much sweetness, too much delight. It was a torment to put her away from him, to deny himself that delight, but he did so.

'Goodnight, Harriet,' he said . . . and

leaned across to open the car door for her.

Briefly, she hesitated, surprised and dismayed and foolishly disappointed . . . but he was already switching on the ignition and he did not look at her again.

Puzzled and a little angry, Harriet let herself into the flat . . . and within ten minutes was between the cool sheets of her bed. She lay still, the light out, suddenly sure that she would not sleep at all for what remained of the night.

She did not know that the strange malaise of heart and mind and body was born of frustration. She scarcely realized the extent of the feelings that David Mellish had aroused in her that night. She only knew that she had wanted him to kiss her and he had failed to do so . . . and she felt that she had been slighted! She only knew that she had been anxious for him to arrange another meeting and he had not made any mention of seeing her again . . . and now she was oddly afraid that it was no more than a casual flirtation on his part and that he had dismissed her already. Had she disappointed him? Had she bored him? Was she too inexperienced, too unsophisticated, for his taste? Had she been too eager, too naively anxious to advance their friendship, too swift to assume that he liked her as much as she liked him?

Her face flamed in the darkness . . . She did like him, so much — but perhaps it had been a mistake to betray it. He was a very different man to Warren who demanded that a woman should show her affection with every word, every glance, every touch of her hand. Warren took with both hands and she had fallen easily into the way of giving. She realized with sudden, sharp clarity that if he had once kindled that sweet, fierce fire within her being then she would have given him very much more — and thought wryly that there was no virtue in resistance when surrender did not offer any temptation!

Her heart suddenly shrank at the thought that David had known how she felt . . . and found it impossible to respond. He had put her away from him in quite unmistakable rejection . . . and driven away without a glance, a wave of his hand or any indication that he wanted to see her again.

The black misery of humiliation swept over her and she decided then and there that she would never go out with him again if he did ask her! She was safer with Warren who did not threaten to sweep her off her feet into foolish loving . . .

★ ★ ★

David knew instantly that the flat was not empty although it was in darkness . . . and the faint, familiar perfume came wafting towards him as she stirred in the deep chair.

He switched on a lamp and she stretched her slim, lithe body and ran her fingers through the short chestnut curls and smiled at him, sleepily sure that he must be pleased to see her. 'Darling David,' she said softly. 'I thought you weren't coming home, after all.'

He bent to kiss the soft, smooth cheek . . . and she twined her hands about his neck and held him down with sudden urgency in every line of her body. David stifled a sigh. 'What is it?' he asked gently but he knew the answer.

'I get so lonely, David,' she said quietly.

'Yes, I know,' he said with compassionate understanding and kissed the soft mouth . . . but it was not the kiss of a lover nor the kiss of a husband and she pushed him away abruptly.

'You know . . . but you no longer care,' she said wryly.

David straightened and looked down at her, a frown in his blue eyes. She did not want him but she could not let him go completely . . . and perhaps in her own way she still loved him. Certainly she still needed him and he found it impossible to cut her out of his life.

Geraldine was a law unto herself and she lived life as she would — and her compulsion to be free of all ties had been one of the factors which led to their divorce. But at the same time the woman who demanded absolute freedom for herself could not grant the same right to anyone who had played a part, however small, in her life. She clung to old friends, past lovers, even the ex-husband whose name she refused to relinquish long after she regretted taking it for her own. She needed desperately to know what was happening to those who had once been important to her . . . and to have them know what was happening in her life. It had always seemed a harmless desire and David was sufficiently fond of Geraldine to accept her continued place in his life . . . and she never attempted to interfere or implied resentment of any of the women who had briefly taken her place throughout the years.

'I care much more than you realize,' he said lightly but sincerely. 'I'm very concerned about you.'

With one of her rapid changes of mood, she leaped up to throw her arms about him in an impulsive hug. 'You're still the nicest man I know,' she said warmly. 'Darling David, I *was* a fool to divorce you!'

There was the familiar wistfulness in her tone and it was a regret she frequently voiced but he knew that the mere hint of a permanent relationship with any man caused her to extricate herself swiftly from an affair. She could not be happy without the freedom she guarded so jealously . . . and yet she found little happiness in life for all her freedom.

'Weren't you?' he said gently, teasing.

He held her quietly, his cheek resting on her curls, an ache in his heart that the woman in his arms was the wrong woman . . .

There was not even the hint of

passion in his embrace and his lips were unresponsive when she reached up to touch them with her own, tentatively. Geraldine drew away slightly and searched his face, a shadow touching her eyes. Of all the men in her life, no one stirred her senses as he still could but she was wise enough to accept that physical attraction was no foundation for happiness.

When little more than boy and girl, they had married on the strength of physical attraction and soon discovered that a very necessary degree of love was lacking in their relationship. Perhaps a kind of loving might have grown with time but in her view life was too short to be wasted in a loveless marriage even with someone as dear and understanding as David. He had agreed to the divorce she wanted, knowing that only his pride would suffer — and throughout the years he had many times blessed her wisdom in freeing them both from that disastrous marriage.

With a little sigh, Geraldine drew away and turned to pick up the coat which she had thrown across a chair. 'Time to go home,' she said lightly.

He knew she wanted to stay, knew she needed the comfort and reassurance that she only found with him because he would let her go without reproach or protest when morning came. But he only wanted Harriet and no other woman could ease the longing in his blood.

By the door, she paused and looked back at him, a little smile in her eyes. 'Is she *very* nice, David?'

He suddenly knew why she had let herself into the flat to wait for him . . . somewhere, she had seen him with Harriet and she was interested, as always, in any woman who interested him. She was terrified, too, that he would marry again and be lost to her entirely, he thought with wry compassion for her muddled emotions. She was a woman who had never really known what she wanted . . . but she was consistent in her reluctance to let him go completely, he thought ruefully.

'I think so but you must decide for yourself when you meet her,' he returned smoothly.

'You're poaching on Warren's preserves,' she said abruptly.

David laughed. 'The boot's usually on the other foot!' That was true for Warren seemed to delight in pursuing any woman who happened to attract David's attention . . . and throughout the years there had always been a kind of light-hearted rivalry between them. But although he laughed and returned a light answer to Geraldine's words, there was anxiety in his heart for Warren had a way with women and, having seen Harriet in his company and witnessed her eager response to his friend's charm and personality, he feared that she was already a little in love.

7

Harriet was on her way to a party and her heart was bumping with excitement. It was not the first party she had been to since coming to London, by any means . . . but it was her first opportunity to meet Polly Prior who was giving the party that evening. She had heard a great deal about the parties that the famous novelist liked to throw . . . parties that had been known to last for days at a time.

As the car ate up the miles, Harriet tried to convince herself that it was not the thought of seeing David again that was causing her heart to behave so foolishly. But he must be there, she told herself hopefully.

She had not seen or heard anything from him since her one and only date with him . . . and she had been so determined not to give it a thought that she had watched for the postman every morning and jumped out of her skin every time the telephone rang and carefully not looked for him while noting his absence from every restaurant, every club, every theatre and every party that she visited in the meantime. She told herself that his obvious lack of interest did not bother her at all . . . and ached for the merest glimpse of him.

It was all so silly. She was not the least bit in love with him, she told herself firmly. She scarcely knew him. No one could fall in love on the strength of one brief meeting in Calderwick and one evening that had seemed a sandwich of disaster with a brief kind of ecstasy in the middle! But he was etched very clearly on her mind . . . and the mere thought of the smile that could warm his very blue eyes could make her weak with longing.

She was going to the party with Warren, of course. She had been out with him almost every night and his attentiveness made her the envy of a great many women and the determined pursuit of a great many men. But Harriet did not notice the envy and she was resolute in refusing all other invitations. She liked Warren and she enjoyed his company and he had been very good to her . . . and the only other man she wanted to be with had apparently forgotten her existence!

Warren was conscious of her excitement but unaware of its cause. He glanced at her with affectionate amusement in his eyes. She was such a child . . . and so enchanting in her unspoiled enjoyment of life.

She did not seem to know that she ought to be flattered by his continued interest . . . but no other woman had held it so firmly and so long with so little reward. For she was quite determined in her resistance to his lovemaking . . . and very often she would pull out of his arms and utter some totally unconnected remark which proved her complete lack of response to his kisses and caresses. It was frustrating and infuriating when he wanted her so desperately . . . and with every day that passed he came nearer to loving her wholeheartedly. He told himself wryly that unless he took care he would find himself thinking of marriage . . . but that prospect no longer filled him with instinctive dismay. Being married to Harriet might be the best thing that could happen in his life! But he did not think she was holding out for marriage. In fact he often doubted that she cared for him at all. She was obviously fond of him but that was not loving . . . and Warren felt it would be ironic if the one woman he was destined to love with all his heart proved to be the one woman who could resist the urge to love him in return!

The party was in full swing when they reached the big house with its lawns sweeping down to the river's edge. Many of the guests had already overflowed into the delightful gardens on the warm summer evening. Music and the sound of happy voices and laughter wafted on the air . . . and Polly Prior held court in the black and white splendour of her lovely drawing-room.

Warren was one of her favourites and she greeted him warmly and rebuked him for neglecting her in recent weeks . . . and Harriet looked with interest at the woman whose glowing beauty had taken her by surprise. The flowing folds of the white gown she wore billowed in the slight breeze from the terrace. The rich auburn hair was piled high on her head and diamonds nestled among the thick curls. The very blue eyes reminded Harriet forcibly of David and caused her heart to quicken a fraction and she instinctively glanced about her in the hope of seeing him. But the room was crowded and if he was present he was hidden among the mass of people.

Polly smiled warmly and with genuine interest as Warren introduced the young woman that Geraldine had described at some length and David appeared so reluctant to discuss although he admitted to knowing and liking her.

She held out her hand and said in her rich, unforgettable voice: 'How do you do? I'm delighted to meet you, my dear. Sit down and talk to me . . . I shall lose you in this crowd and I want to talk to you about Calderwick. It used to be my home, too, you know.'

Harriet's heart leaped a little at this unmistakable evidence that David had talked to his mother about her. In response to that almost royal command, she sat down on the black velvet sofa beside her hostess, warmed by the smile that was so much like David's that she took an immediate liking to the beautiful and very famous novelist.

Polly was very curious about the unknown newcomer to the London scene who seemed to have neither beauty nor wealth nor family to recommend her and yet had attracted so much attention. It could not be merely because Warren was interested in the girl . . . there had been far too many women in his life. So she must have some quality, some degree of charm, that caught and held the attention — and Polly, meeting the clear directness of those grey eyes and noting the rare sweetness of that expressive mouth and the quiet dignity that sat so naturally on young shoulders, knew immediately that Harriet Burns had an integrity, a simplicity and a strength of character that must appeal to others as much as it appealed to her . . .

'I gather that my son has turned you out of your home,' she said lightly, smiling.

Harriet laughed. 'Not exactly! It was originally my aunt's house and when she died I was quite happy to leave it for London!' she said frankly.

'I must have known your aunt but I really can't remember . . . it's a long time ago now, of course. I do remember the house — it's just across the road from the Vicarage, isn't it?

David was born in that Vicarage — did he tell you?'

David, arriving late, came into the room and approached, unnoticed. He caught the words and said lightly from behind Harriet: 'I expect I bored the lady at length with my memories of Calderwick, Mama!' As Harriet turned swiftly, startled by his voice into a betrayal of delight, he said easily: 'How are you, Harriet?' He nodded to Warren and bent to kiss his mother. 'You look very beautiful, Mama,' he said, meaning it.

Warren was shaken and immediately suspicious of the glow that had leaped to Harriet's eyes. He was suddenly sick with dismay, suddenly understanding the baffling and hurtful lack of response in her to his desire. Yet he had been sure that she was virtually indifferent to David's existence . . . he told himself that he had misinterpreted the faint colour that crept into her face and misunderstood the sudden warmth in her lovely eyes — and tried to believe it.

'I thought you weren't coming,' David,' Polly said in light reproach. 'You're very late!'

'I've been very busy.' He had been away for some days, staying at the pub in Calderwick while he supervised the start of the building work on the house and renewed his acquaintance with the copse and the river that cut the village in half and the old church and its memorial tablet to his father.

He had gone away in the hope of putting Harriet out of his mind for her affair with Warren showed every sign of lasting. He had disciplined himself to resist the temptation to get in touch with her but the longing to see her had not lessened with the passing days. Now he knew that she was in his heart and in his mind for ever . . . and it was hard to greet her as though she was no more than a casual acquaintance.

Harriet was very conscious of him, standing behind the sofa . . . she was very conscious of his hand, resting on the back of the sofa only inches away from her shoulder. She ached to know his touch even while she despised herself for such weakness. The sound of his voice had set her heart leaping in her breast and the sight of him, tall and very handsome in the midnight blue tuxedo with the pale blue of his dress shirt emphasizing the warm brown of his skin and the very deep blue of his eyes, had confirmed abruptly that it was possible to love a man that she scarcely knew.

The revelation left her breathless and speechless . . . and she did not even dare to look at him again for fear he should read in her eyes all that was in her heart. For he must not be allowed to suspect that she loved him. She could not throw herself at his head and his light, careless greeting combined with his completely indifferent silence of several days indicated quite clearly that he would not welcome the least betrayal of her feelings.

Warren reached for her hand and drew her to her feet and she smiled up at him in sudden, warm gratitude for his presence and the affection which could provide a convincing camouflage for her heart's foolish behaviour. Warren, seeing only that swift smile and the warmth in her eyes and the readiness of her response to his touch, was reassured and relieved . . . and he realized in that moment how much it meant that she should not care more for David or any other man then for him.

'We ought to circulate,' he said lightly. 'Polly darling, we mustn't monopolise you a moment longer. We'll come back to you later.'

Warren led Harriet away, a possessive arm about that slender waist . . . and David looked after them until they were engulfed by the press of people in the room. He sat down beside his mother and smiled a little wryly when she suddenly covered his hand with her own in an unmistakable gesture of sympathy.

She was so rarely demonstrative that he knew immediately that in some way he had betrayed himself.

'She's lovely,' Polly said gently, touching delicately on the sensitivity of his feelings with a mother's compassion and concern. She knew his love and longing for the woman he had scarcely greeted . . . and could not explain how she knew. 'A lovely girl . . . '

'I thought you would like her,' David said quietly.

'Yes, I do. But one can never get to know people properly at parties. You must bring her to see me another day, David. Will you do that?'

'Perhaps . . . '

She patted his hand lightly. 'You're in love with her, David.' It was a statement of fact, spoken softly.

'I love her,' he amended.

She nodded. 'Yes,' she said, understanding. 'I loved only one man in my life. But I've been in love many times . . . without even liking the man very often. I'm glad you know the

130

difference, darling. What are you going to do?'

'There doesn't seem to be much I can do,' he said without self-pity. 'She's very much involved with Warren . . . I daresay you've heard all about it on the grapevine?'

'It had been mentioned,' Polly said lightly. 'But do you think she cares so much for him?'

'Yes, I do,' he returned firmly . . . for he really did believe that Harriet was in love and hoping to marry his friend. Only a few moments before, she had gone off with Warren, looking up at him with obvious admiration and affection in her eyes . . . but she had granted him the merest of smiles and never a word despite the fact that not so very long ago he had held her close with longing in his heart and in his blood that she must have sensed.

He suspected that she had completely forgotten the evening they had spent together . . . and why should she remember it when all her thoughts, all her emotions, all her time were so taken up with Warren who was determined on conquest. For all he knew, the man's persuasive charm had already won him what he wanted, David thought grimly . . . and wondered why he had made a special effort to get back to town in time for his mother's party when he had known very well that seeing Harriet in such circumstances would cause him torment . . .

Harriet was determined to enjoy the party if only so that Warren should not be disappointed by her lack of spirits. But it was difficult to be gay and light-hearted and amusing when she saw David talking easily to other women, dancing with other women, smiling and raising his glass to other women . . . and studiously avoiding her. But that was not strictly correct . . . he was not avoiding her so much as ignoring her! He was so indifferent to her that he was simply not aware of her unless she crossed his line of vision . . . and then he would acknowledge her with the faintest of smiles.

She was quite incapable of flirting or she might have set out to show David Mellish that she was not at all concerned about his lack of interest. Her heart was like a lump of lead hanging heavily in her breast but she made the effort to seem her usual self. Hankering for a man who did not want her was not going to get her anywhere, she told herself firmly . . . and she ought to be grateful that she was wanted by someone as nice and as attractive as Warren.

Gratitude, she thought wryly . . . it seemed that she was destined never to escape it. All her life she had been grateful to Aunt Sarah for the roof over her head, the clothes on her back, the food in her mouth . . . now she was grateful to Rae who was not urging her to find a flat of her own because she knew how difficult it was to find anywhere at a reasonable rent and grateful to Warren whose affection and friendship and company meant a very great deal to a shy country mouse trying to make her own way in life for the first time. At least she did not have to be grateful to David who unaccountably had whisked her heart out of her own possession ... it seemed very likely that she would have nothing to thank him for but heartache!

Yet she could not resist the opportunity of a few precious moments with him when it offered. Warren was deep in conversation with one of his friends and Harriet wandered to the edge of the terrace, a trifle bored. Looking down to the gleaming ribbon of water at the end of the garden, she suddenly realized that David was standing alone at the river's edge. With a swift glance for Warren who was too involved in the discussion to realize that she was no longer by his side, she caught up her long skirts and went down the stone steps and across the lawns to join David, scarcely caring that he must wonder why she sought him out . . . and the rustle of the stiff taffeta of her dress caught his quick ear as she approached. He turned and her heart lurched as he smiled in swift and spontaneous greeting.

'How lovely the river looks in the moonlight,' Harriet said breathlessly, suddenly at a loss to know what to say to him.

David looked down at her, thinking how lovely she looked in the moonlight . . . beautiful and very dear to him in the deep rose gown with her pale hair banded smoothly about the proud head and her face illuminated softly and very prettily by the moon that sailed so serenely across the night sky.

'Yes . . . very lovely,' he said, wholly indifferent to the beauty of the river in that moment.

Harriet laughed shakily for there was a very disturbing admiration in his eyes. 'Well, look at it!' she exclaimed in light reproach.

'I've seen it many times. You are much more beautiful,' he told her, taking her hand and tucking it beneath his arm as though it belonged there. He did not mean to question her unexpected approach to him. It was enough that she had sought him out and that there was warm friendliness in her smile and a very natural ease of understanding between them as they stood beside the quietly-flowing water.

Harriet hugged the quiet words to her heart even while common-sense insisted that they were empty flirtation from a man who enjoyed the company of women while relentlessly avoiding emotional entanglement. He was very attractive, very personable, very much a man of the world . . . it was inevitable that he had many women friends. She would be a fool to take any of his attentions too seriously or to heed anything he might say to her, however flattering. So she was a fool, she thought wryly . . . but she would remember and cherish the words he had just uttered.

Her hand rested lightly on his arm

while they stood together, talking quietly and of the merest common-places but talking as friends who liked each other's company and conversation. Harriet was content. She might ache to know his arms about her, yearn for the magic of his kiss and the ecstasy of his embrace . . . but there was satisfaction in knowing that they could be together and close with a different and perhaps more enduring kind of intimacy . . .

8

Warren was aware that Harriet was no longer by his side but he assumed that she had gone off to dance with one of the men who had been so attentive that evening and might have seized an opportunity to whisk her away while he talked to his friends.

He went into the house to look for her. The crowd was thinning with the lateness of the hour and it was almost time that he took Harriet home for she had to go to the boutique in the morning as usual and he had an early appointment with a client. But she was nowhere to be seen and none of his friends could tell him where she was and enquiries from other people brought blank looks for the most part for Harriet was still a stranger to many of them.

He returned to the terrace, fully

expecting her to be looking for him by this time.

A woman moved out of the shadows towards him with the deliberate intention of delaying him, knowing that he was looking for Harriet Burns and knowing where she was to be found. She moved towards him slowly, smiling, very sure of herself . . . and Warren paused and ran his eyes over the lithe body in the backless and virtually topless black dress with instinctive male response to the sensuality in her approach.

She had the kind of animal magnetism that could stop any man in his tracks, he thought wryly, momentarily forgetting his search for Harriet. He moistened his suddenly dry lips. 'Hallo, Geraldine . . . how are you?' he greeted her coolly but his blood was hot in his veins as he looked down at her.

'Very bored,' she drawled. She moved even closer and smiled up at him with unmistakable provocation in her eyes. 'You used to be very skilled at alleviating boredom, Warren,' she said softly.

He was very tempted to linger in the shadows and taste the sweetness of her lips . . . but he knew from past experience that he would only despise himself for the weakness of wanting her — and besides there was Harriet to consider, he suddenly remembered. He touched her cheek with his fingers in a careless caress.

'Not tonight, Geraldine,' he said lightly. 'I'm looking for someone . . . a fair girl in a pinkish dress. She was out here with me a few minutes ago . . . did you happen to notice her?'

Geraldine raised an amused eyebrow, quite untroubled by the rebuff. 'Darling, there must be a dozen fair girls in pinkish dresses roaming about the place! As a description that's a miserable failure! I'd hate to think how you'd describe me to a stranger!'

He chuckled. 'A fascinating charmer in a dressless strap,' he told her promptly, a little mischievously. 'What is that thing you're not wearing tonight, my sweet . . . a delightful concoction that you just threw on — and missed!'

She laughed softly. 'It seems to have had disappointingly little impact so far,' she said with mock regret.

'Poor darling!' he commiserated. 'You shouldn't hide out here all evening . . . why, I didn't even know you were here!'

'Your fair lady takes up all your attention,' she told him lightly. 'I don't know how you were careless enough to mislay her . . . but she's down by the river — with David.' There was the faintest hint of malice in the slow, sleepy drawl and she watched the narrowing of his eyes with some satisfaction. 'Isn't it odd how you always want the same women . . . you and David? Sometimes I think you do it deliberately, darling . . . if you're always getting back at him for taking me away from you.'

'Water under the bridge, Geraldine,'

he said, a little harshly, for he did not care to be reminded that in his university days he had been heavily and foolishly in love with the girl who had preferred David and married him only to regret it.

Her eyes widened suddenly. 'It was a joke,' she said slowly. 'But now I'm not so sure! Did you really care so much, Warren?'

There was something in her voice, a certain concern, a faint regret, that abruptly penetrated his defences. In all the years he had never allowed her to know how much he had cared . . . oh, he had recovered much quicker than he had supposed at the time and by the time she was free of her marriage to David he had completely lost interest. Pride alone would have forbidden him to love her again and with greater maturity came the understanding that while his body still wanted her she could never own his heart.

'First love hits hard,' he said wryly, impulsively admitting a truth he had concealed for a very long time.

'Oh, but you never loved me!' Geraldine exclaimed impetuously.

'Oh, but I did,' he said with a rueful smile. 'It felt like love at the time, anyway.'

'Well, I never knew,' she retorted with a hint of resentment.

'You might have known if you'd had eyes for anyone but David,' he pointed out lightly.

'I took David because you didn't want me!'

'You took David because you were desperate to marry someone — anyone,' he said bluntly.

'I wanted you — but you weren't the marrying kind,' she reminded him, her smile not quite reaching her eyes.

He regarded her thoughtfully. 'I remember,' he said quietly. 'You were rushing me — and I wasn't ready to talk about marriage. Then I introduced you to David . . . and within a month you married him! Now you expect me to believe that you were really in love with me all the time! It's too late, Geraldine . . . and we are two very different people now.'

'And you're in love with Harriet Burns,' she said flatly.

He smiled. 'Am I?'

'People are saying that you mean to marry her,' she told him coolly.

'People will say anything,' he said dryly.

'What about David?' she asked abruptly.

He had moved away from her to the edge of the stone steps. The gardens were rapidly emptying for a light, chill breeze had sprung up out of nowhere. In the distance, he could see two people standing by the edge of the river . . . a man and a woman, standing close together, too close for his liking. His hands clenched involuntarily. 'What about David?' he echoed stiffly.

'Perhaps he also means to marry her.'

Warren shrugged. 'Then may the best man win!' he said lightly and ran down the steps and strode purposefully towards the river.

Geraldine looked after him and there was a pain like a knife in her breast. Too many men had walked away from her with that easy, careless indifference. Too many men had found it possible to dismiss her after an affair. Too many men had wanted her only briefly . . . and although one experience of marriage had set her against it there was an aching loneliness in her way of life and a terrible futility in reaching out for happiness that she knew could not last.

Perhaps everything might have been very different if she had known twelve years before that Warren cared for her. But the handsome, ambitious young man who was never without a pretty girl on his arm had dated her only a few times and made no protest when David began to turn up at the same parties and monopolized her attention. Perhaps she had been piqued by Warren's resolute declaration that he would never marry and that no woman was worth the sacrifice of his freedom . . . but she had encouraged David and eventually convinced herself that she loved him enough to marry him — and Warren had turned up at their wedding with an even prettier girl on his arm and a careless indifference to losing Geraldine to his best friend.

Was it really twelve years, she asked herself with a sense of shock? Twelve years since she had been young and hopelessly in love and snatching at marriage with David only to discover that he could not ease that terrible, persistent ache in her heart. It still persisted, all these years later, but she had almost forgotten its cause . . . now Warren had reminded her just why she skipped from one man to another and fought shy of any permanent association. It was a desperate search for the kind of happiness and ease of mind and body that only one man could give her . . . and still he did not want her for all the empty talk of having loved her once!

Warren strode across the lawn to the point where Harriet stood with David . . . and he was annoyed with his friend for failing to realize that she might be cold in this sudden breeze. They turned at his approach and he fancied that Harriet looked a little guilty . . . and so she should, he thought angrily, for there was no need for furtive liaisons in the moonlight. If she wanted David than she had only to say so!

'I've been looking for you,' he said, more curtly than he had intended.

'Well, you've found me,' Harriet returned lightly. 'But I didn't realize I was lost!' She smiled at him but she was a little dismayed by his obvious anger. She did not think that she had done anything wrong in slipping away to talk to David for a few minutes but it was apparent that Warren disapproved. She supposed she should be flattered that he was sufficiently fond of her to resent her interest in any other man. But she did not want him to be jealous or to feel at all possessive towards her for that would mean that he was beginning to care too deeply and Harriet knew she must disappoint him. 'David has been looking after me very well,' she added, maintaining her light hold on his arm and looking up at him with a swift, sweet smile. It seemed a golden opportunity to offer David a hint of warm encouragement and to point out gently to Warren that he must not be too proprietorial where she was concerned.

Warren's eyes narrowed suddenly. 'I hope you aren't taking him too seriously,' he said lightly, clapping his friend on the shoulder. 'He always chases my women! Don't you, David? It's sheer force of habit — we've been rivals since boyhood!'

A shadow touched her eyes at the words which lumped her so airily with a host of other women who had meant little to either of them . . . and she wondered if Warren had deliberately set out to destroy the magic of those few moments with David. She waited, a little anxiously, for him to deny the light-hearted accusation.

David met the challenge in his friend's eyes. He could not mistake the warning which was more of an urgent plea — and he could not blame Warren for wanting Harriet. To know her was to love her, after all! Warren had been the light-hearted lover of many women but that did not mean that he was incapable of loving deeply.

Harriet had sought him out, walked and talked with him in seeming enjoyment of his company and attention, smiled at him with apparent encouragement . . . and briefly he rebelled against Warren's open claim to her in the light words which defied him to deny that his interest was anything more than a casual, careless rivalry for her affection. Then he recalled Harriet's responses to his friend, the warm sweetness of her expression when she looked at him, her eagerness to spend almost every free moment in his company . . . and compared it with the mild, friendly warmth of her attitude to himself. A woman in love might use any means to achieve what she wanted — and Harriet was the kind of woman who would believe that loving was synonymous with marriage. Perhaps she sought to use the interest he could not conceal to urge Warren into marriage, David thought wryly . . . it was feminine strategy that seldom took into account the impact of such behaviour on the loser's mind and heart!

But her happiness was all-important to him — and perhaps he could play some small part in ensuring it for the woman he loved.

So he laughed and said with equal lightness: 'It proves that we both have excellent taste, my friend.'

Warren put an arm about Harriet's slight shoulders and drew her towards him, smiling down at her with his heart in his eyes . . . and David allowed her hand to slip from his arm without protest.

Harriet knew, quite instinctively, that she was being handed over with his blessing, so to speak . . . and it was a clear indication even without those careless words that his interest in her was merely superficial. She was so dismayed, so hurt, so angry that she hated both of them in that moment. How dared they decide her future between themselves! How dared Warren assume that proprietorial air when she had never given him the least right to do so! How dared David dismiss her so airily when he must know that she wanted him! He was either blind or a fool if he did not know, she thought furiously, quite forgetting how practised she was in schooling her innermost emotions.

'I'm cold,' she said abruptly, shivering . . . and it was the coldness of despair that touched her. The despair of knowing that she loved and would always love a man who did not want her . . .

It was David who promptly took off

his jacket and thrust it about her bare shoulders . . . and she thanked him a little stiffly and walked between them to the house, forcing herself to join in the exchange of remarks while she clutched his coat to her and wished it was his embrace that warmed her.

Later, just as they were leaving the party, she saw him dancing with a woman whose dress was so revealing that Harriet was a little shocked, still not quite accustomed to the pace of life that was so different to Calderwick. She was an attractive woman . . . and it was obvious that David was attracted, she thought bitterly. For he held the woman very close and her arms were about his neck as though they embraced rather than danced and the movement of her slender body was seductive rather than rhythmic as they moved about the big room to the music . . . and she turned away, sick with an emotion she did not analyse immediately as jealousy.

She was a fool to think that David Mellish was worthy of her love, she told herself bitterly ... he was just a womanizer, a charmer, a selfish and superficial man who took what he wanted with both hands and gave nothing in return. There were too many men like him in the world ... and it was just her luck to have fallen in love with one of them! Well, she would make it her business to fall promptly out of love ... and it would be a long time before she made a fool of herself again!

Warren could not help but be aware of her silent misery. He brought the car to a halt in a quiet road and turned to her ... and touched his fingers to the wetness of her cheeks. 'Harriet, you're crying!' he exclaimed in swift concern.

She shook her head. 'No, I'm not!' Her voice was muffled with tears. Warren smiled with wry tenderness and drew her into his arms. 'Tell me, darling ... '

She struggled with her heaviness of heart. She did not want him or anyone else to know the cause of that foolish ache in her heart. She lay in his arms, grateful for their reassurance, her spirits lifting slightly in response to his affection and concern. 'It's nothing,' she said, forcing back the tears. 'A little foolishness. I expect I'm just tired . . . too many late nights, probably!' she added with a little laugh.

He held her, stroking the soft hair. He knew . . . but every fibre of his being fought against that instinctive knowledge. Yet he said quietly: 'Is it David?'

Briefly, her whole body tensed . . . and then she relaxed against him. 'No.' The lie was not easy for her and she could only bring out that one brief word of denial.

Warren knew that she lied . . . but she was in his arms and he told himself that he could teach her to love him and forget this foolish fancy for another man. He did not mean to lose his love a second time to his friend . . . and he refused to believe that David could love and want her as much as he did. He had let her go, without protest . . . and he would soon find consolation in another woman's arms!

Holding Harriet, he longed to speak of his love for her but his instinct warned him that this was not the moment. Instead, he kissed her and the eager response was reassuring. He murmured her name with tenderness and kissed her again, trying to ignore the suspicion that she sought to ease her longing for David in his arms.

Harriet gave the sweetness of her lips and knew she could never give him the love that he deserved. Compassion stirred for she had tasted the bitterness of rejection and knew the despair of loving and longing in vain.

She had believed that love was a rainbow, a promise of no more loneliness and only happiness to come. Like a child, she had reached out in the belief that the gold of eternal bliss was to be found at the end of the rainbow . . . but it had slipped through her fingers like fairy dust.

9

The party went on into the small hours and David, in reckless, heartsore mood, sought solace in Geraldine's company. She knew and encouraged his need of her for she was also sick at heart and anxious for a brief respite from the urgency of wanting a man who would never want her.

As they drank and talked and danced in close embrace, David told himself that his ache for Harriet could be assuaged and forgotten in the arms of another woman . . . and why not Geraldine who was lovely and desirable and willing. He needed to dispel the persistent image of Harriet going off so happily with Warren . . . he drank again and caught Geraldine to him and swept her into the dance.

In his arms, Geraldine indulged in the foolish fantasy that it was Warren's arms that encircled her, yet sudden tenderness stirred as she looked up at David. She was very fond of him and she wondered wryly, as she had wondered so often, if they might have made something of their marriage if she had not been so determined on her freedom.

David, his eyes closed as he held her close to him, placed his lips gently against her hair, murmuring a name. Not her name, she realized with a pang . . . and wondered if he had also fantasized while dancing with her. Had she been Harriet Burns to him while he held her? She reminded herself that she had no right to that instinctive protest for she was equally guilty. She did not love David any more than he loved her . . . they had merely come together and clung together out of mutual need for comfort and reassurance.

Geraldine drew away and David followed her from the dance floor, looking at her thoughtfully. At thirty, she was still a beautiful woman . . . more beautiful than she had been when they married and as a successful fashion writer she was reaping the fruits of her determination to put her career before their marriage. But she was not a happy woman and he wondered if he should have refused the divorce she demanded and tried very much harder to love the girl he had married. They had both taken the easy way out, he thought ruefully — and now, twelve years later, they both had empty hands . . .

Words leaped impulsively to David's mind as he looked at her and with equal impulsiveness he spoke them: 'We ought to get married, Geraldine.'

She stared — and sat down suddenly on the edge of a chair. 'Because . . . ?' she demanded lightly, mockingly.

'Because of many things,' he said soberly. Perhaps instinct rather than impulse had been behind the thought because it seemed an excellent solution to her loneliness and the emptiness of his own life and he went on steadily: 'I think we need each other, don't you?'

She laughed dryly. 'If I agreed we'd certainly *deserve* each other! Pair of fools we would be to make the same mistake a second time. David, you're a dear and I love you but I certainly won't marry you!'

'Why not?'

She searched his face, wondering. 'You're serious, David,' she suddenly discovered, astonished.

'Yes, I think I am.'

She was silent, considering his words. Was it the answer? Could they be happy, after all . . . twelve years later? They had rushed into a youthful, disastrous marriage — but basically they had felt they belonged together — and perhaps they did! Perhaps her longing for Warren was not love at all but habit! Perhaps her real love was David who was certainly very dear to her. But David . . . what could be his motive in wanting them to re-marry? Sheer loneliness, perhaps . . . he was a man who needed a wife, home and children and only his integrity and his instinct had prevented him from a second marriage all these years. David would not take second-best, very wisely . . . if he did not love wholeheartedly he would not marry any woman.

His amazing proposal was just a temporary weakness on his part, Geraldine knew . . . he really wanted Harriet Burns who did not seem to want him! Geraldine thought unhappily that she knew exactly how he felt. She was briefly tempted to the same kind of weakness. For her life was very empty and lonely at times and she had found that a successful career and plenty of money and a full social life did not compensate for the lack of a man who truly loved her and provided the complete fulfilment of all her dreams. She was a woman like any other and she desperately wanted to share her life with someone who really cared about her . . .

'It isn't the answer, David,' she said slowly, not too surely. 'It didn't work before and it wouldn't work now.'

'We were children before,' he pointed out, a trifle impatiently. He was sure that he was right. Harriet was beyond his reach — but he and Geraldine could surely find some degree of happiness together. They liked each other and that was important. They had much in common and they talked the same language. As sensible, reasonable adults they ought to be able to make a marriage work . . . and because they had been married to each other before they would know all the pitfalls to avoid!

Geraldine rose. 'I have to go now,' she said truthfully and a little thankfully for it might be all too easy to surrender to the warm persuasion in his smiling eyes if she stayed. 'It's awfully late and I'm tired. David, I don't know . . . perhaps you're right. Perhaps we *do* need each other. Let me think it over for a few days. We don't have to rush into anything, after all . . . not this time.'

He called her back with the soft,

urgent use of her name and she turned to look at him with a question in her eyes. 'I do want you, Geraldine,' he said quietly.

'Yes . . . ' she said doubtfully. 'But wanting and loving are two very different things, darling David! I want you — but I think I love you too much to take you!'

Throughout the next busy day, Geraldine mulled over that astonishing proposal . . . and the more she thought about it the more tempted she felt. She had always guarded her freedom so jealously . . . but abruptly she had realized that freedom was no such thing when she was deeply in thrall to her urgent love and longing for Warren. Perhaps her only hope of knowing any happiness at all lay with David. Yet she was afraid of damaging their very precious relationship if she married him a second time for out of the ashes of that first, foolish marriage had risen the phoenix of a warm, close friendship which would never fail her. She loved

David dearly . . . but a husband was very different to a good friend!

Late in the afternoon, she paid a visit to the boutique in Knightsbridge that was currently fashionable among the young and trendy, largely owing to her efforts. An impulse to add to her already extensive wardrobe plus the need of copy for her column in a national newspaper coincided with her interest in Harriet Burns who was presently working for Clare. She wanted to know more about the girl who had not only captured Warren's apparently enduring interest but also brought a man like David to his knees with love for her.

In all the years that she had known David she had never seen that particular look in his eyes for any woman . . . not even for herself when they were first married. Harriet Burns obviously had a certain quality that set her above other women . . . but Geraldine, trying to be scrupulously fair, could not analyse what it was. She was not even more than pretty although she had something that attracted a second and perhaps a third glance, Geraldine admitted.

Clare welcomed her warmly for she was an old and valued friend. Geraldine talked to her about the new fashions and made copious notes and admired or criticized the clothes that Clare brought for her verdict . . . but she was much more interested in the tall, slender girl who was so patient with a difficult exacting client . . .

Harriet recognized her as soon as she walked in. She might have changed the daring black dress for a chic grey suit but there was no mistaking the soft chestnut curls or the oval and rather distinctive beauty of the face that had haunted her dreams all night.

It was Harriet's first experience of a jealousy that could twist one's heart with pain and stir black thoughts in the recesses of one's mind . . . and it came as something of a shock to feel such dislike for a complete stranger. But it hurt badly to recall that so soon after walking with her by the river, implying a warmth and an intimacy in their relationship that was very precious to her, David could turn his attentions so pointedly to another woman. And such a woman . . . beautiful, sophisticated, daringly dressed to display her physical charms to their best advantage, provocatively sure of herself and deliberately setting her cap at David! And he had been so taken up with her that he had not even noticed when Harriet left the party, she thought unhappily . . . and could not have cared a snap of his fingers that she had left on Warren's arm!

She tried to tell herself that she was expecting far too much from a man who was little more than a stranger and was merely being courteously attentive to her because circumstances had dictated their association. After all, if he had not bought Calderwick House and she had merely met him through her friendship with Warren, he would probably not have given her a second thought — and why should he?

Her foolish heart might cling to the hope that he liked and admired her, was attracted to her, would be more attentive to her if it was not for her friendship with Warren . . . but common-sense scoffed at the fancy. If he cared he would not let Warren stand in his way even though they were friends! If he cared he would not flaunt an interest in another woman under her nose!

'Who is that . . . ?' she whispered to one of the other girls at the first opportunity.

Sally glanced briefly at Clare and her companion. 'A fashion writer for the *Echo*,' she returned indifferently, turning back to whisk through the rail of dresses. 'She's given us a lot of publicity lately. That suit is ours — it really looks good on her, doesn't it?' She picked out a dress and surveyed it critically. 'I can't think of her name . . . Geraldine something-or-other . . . '

Geraldine something-or-other looked in their direction as though she had caught the sound of her name. She smiled, murmured something to Clare and moved towards Harriet who felt oddly on the defensive despite the unmistakable friendliness in the woman's eyes.

'Hallo there,' Geraldine said lightly, confidently. 'Didn't I see you at Polly's party last night . . . with Warren Hailey?'

'Yes, that's right.'

'I thought I recognized you. Oh, we weren't introduced — it wasn't that kind of party. But I think we must have exchanged a word or two in passing.' She skimmed through the dresses on the rail with a practised eye. 'I'm looking for something interesting,' she said and picked out two of the dresses. 'I'll take these. They have a hint of the Rae Carpenter touch, don't you think?'

'They are adapted copies of dresses she designed for Thelma McCall's new television series,' Harriet said, a little stiffly, envying the other woman's easy confidence.

'Oh, but you know Rae, of course . . . you're staying with her, aren't you?'

'Only temporarily — while I look for a flat,' Harriet explained as she always did but she had already discovered how difficult it was to find suitable rented property in London.

'Oh, you poor girl! It's a hopeless business!' Geraldine exclaimed.

'So I'm finding out,' Harriet said wryly. 'If I can afford a place it turns out to be virtually unfit for human habitation. And if it's the answer to a prayer then I just can't afford it!'

Geraldine nodded. 'Yes, I know,' she sympathized. 'Rents are sky-high!' She smiled suddenly, a little indulgently. 'But your problem will probably solve itself if there's any truth in the rumour that you and Warren are *very* good friends.'

Harriet blushed slightly. 'Friends,'

she said with emphasis. 'Nothing more!'

Geraldine laughed softly. 'For the moment, perhaps. But I won't tease you. If you are really looking for a flat then I may be able to help,' she added, her mind leaping to David's proposal and its possible results. 'No definite promise, of course — but there is a possibility that a friend of mine will be giving up his flat in the near future and it may be just what you're looking for.'

She scarcely knew what urged her to make the suggestion. Something about Harriet Burns that she liked, perhaps . . . or swift relief because her words and manner had implied that she would not rush into marriage with Warren if he should suggest it — and while he remained a bachelor then Geraldine could hug that persistent hope to her heart.

She did not realize the irony of offering David's flat to Harriet in the circumstances for she had not the least suspicion that the girl cared for him. She believed that her interest and affection were centred on Warren for the time being even if she was not thinking of marriage.

Harriet paused in the act of sliding a dress into the gay, chequered box. 'That's very kind of you,' she said warmly, surprised and swift to regret her first dislike of the woman.

'Oh, one does what one can for one's friends,' Geraldine said lightly.

Harriet smiled — and knew that she had been wrong to resent the need for gratitude. Everyone had been so kind to her and now a virtual stranger was anxious to befriend and help her . . . how could she be anything but grateful and touched? It was very easy to be proud and foolishly independent — but it was very wrong to hurt and offend and stand aloof from those who wanted to care about her, protect her, help and guide her. It was wonderful that people did care — and in return she must give affection and interest and concern . . . with a heart filled and overflowing with a gratitude they richly deserved.

In that swift, sweet smile, Geraldine recognized the quality that attracted men so forcibly — and she understood why Harriet Burns was generally liked. She had cause to resent her very existence yet she could not help warming instinctively to the sweetness and sincerity of the girl who had a decided gift for endearing herself.

She picked up the boxes and said brightly: 'I'll keep in touch.' She waggled her fingers in a careless goodbye for Clare who was making a telephone call and smiled once more at Harriet. 'Put the dresses down to my account . . . it's in the name of Mellish. Mrs David Mellish.'

She went out to her waiting car . . . quite unaware that Harriet looked after her, stunned and dismayed by those careless words. She had not intended to be cruel . . . she had simply taken it for granted that Harriet Burns, like almost everyone else, must know all about her long-ago marriage to Warren's friend — and her account with Clare dated back to those days . . .

10

Harriet decided to walk home via the park that evening . . . the long way round that would give her a little time to adjust to the shattering discovery that David was a married man. Her mind and heart were still jarred from the shock of that carelessly-spoken revelation.

It had never occurred to her to wonder about his marital status . . . and no one had ever mentioned the fact of his wife, least of all David himself! She knew that this new world was vastly different to the one she had always known and the ways, manners and behaviour of its inhabitants seemed at times to be totally alien . . . but it was still incredible that a man and his wife could lead such separate lives that a stranger was completely unaware that they were married at all.

She could not blame Rae who probably did not realize her interest in anything and everything that concerned David . . . after all, she had never discussed her love for him with Rae and the one date she had with him must have seemed very platonic and to all intents and purposes she had been deeply involved with Warren ever since she arrived in London. There was absolutely no reason why Rae should have mentioned the fact that David was married . . . and everyone else, including Warren, had probably assumed that she knew.

It was a golden evening, warm and heady with the scents of the beautiful, well-kept flower beds. But Harriet, seeing so many lovers hand in hand as they walked through London's famous park, realized that it had been a mistake to choose this route with its poignant reminders of her foolish love.

She quickened her steps, trying not to see David in every tall, dark-haired man, trying not to compare the happiness of those young and light-hearted lovers with the bleak hopelessness of her own loving. She wondered why she had chosen to love him, someone she scarcely knew, when it would have been so much more sensible to care for Warren. But her heart gave back the prompt answer . . . it had not been choice but destiny! Out of all the men in the world she had been meant to love David . . . the stranger she had known instinctively as her love.

Arriving at the flat, she walked into seeming chaos. Floor, chairs and tables were strewn with lengths of material, paper patterns, sketches, swathes of fabrics and colours, books and magazines and all the other paraphernalia that seemed to be necessary adjuncts to Rae's work.

Rae was sitting at her drawing-board with her dark hair standing on end where she had run her long, clever fingers through the short silky locks a dozen times in desperate search of inspiration.

'Who dropped the bomb!' Harriet exclaimed, amused despite her unhappy heart as she picked her way through the debris.

Rae grinned. 'Oh, I can't be bothered with non-essentials when I'm giving birth,' she returned carelessly. 'I know the place is a mess but I've had the Merrick wedding dumped in my lap . . . Lady Prue's wedding gown and the frocks for the bridesmaids.'

Harriet was not deceived by the throw-away tone. 'But that's marvellous, Rae,' she said warmly and with genuine pleasure at the news. The Merricks were a very wealthy and influential family and the women invariably patronized only the best of the international fashion houses. The wedding that had been arranged between Lady Prudence and a scion of a distinguished family that traced its ancestry back to the Tudors was already being acclaimed as the Wedding of the Year by society columnists . . . and it was a terrific boost to Rae's reputation and career to have been asked to submit designs for the wedding dress.

Rae lifted her thin shoulders in a faint shrug. 'Well, I don't know . . . I usually refuse wedding commissions but Prudence Merrick is a challenge, you must admit,' she said lightly. 'She's such a gawky girl when she isn't on a horse and none of the top-notch couturiers seem to have done much for her so far. I'd like to endow her with a little grace and beauty for one day in her life at least!'

Harriet looked over her friend's shoulder at the almost-completed sketch which was pinned to the drawing-board. 'Oh, I like that!' she exclaimed involuntarily. 'Rae, you're a genius!'

Rae laughed. 'I have my moments,' she said modestly but she was more than satisfied with the results of an afternoon's work. 'I think the Elizabethan ruff is a nice touch, don't you?' Idly, almost doodling, she added a few strokes to the sketch with her pencil . . . and suddenly it came to glowing life and the bride was instantly recognizable.

'She looks just like you,' Harriet said without thinking . . . and could have bitten out her tongue as Rae's face flamed and she ripped the sheet of drawing paper from the board and crumpled it swiftly. 'Oh, Rae . . . ' she said with quick compassion.

'Wishful thinking will out,' Rae said with a painfully wry smile. She rose abruptly and walked to the open window and stood by it, staring across the park that was spread below in green and pleasant panorama.

Harriet regarded her with troubled eyes, discovering that she had been selfish in supposing that she was the only one with a heartache. Caught up in the tumult of her own emotions, she had forgotten all about Rae's involvement with the man she had once planned to marry . . . and Rae was not the kind of person to inflict her problems, personal or otherwise, on anyone else. Yet if Harriet had taken a little time off from her own concerns in the past few weeks she would have realized a new restlessness in Rae, a slightly superficial cheerfulness that was meant to conceal a depression and an unusual preference for her own company of late.

Because Rae was an easy-going, fun-loving attractive girl with a host of friends, a book full of social engagements and a career that was both satisfying and successful, it was too easy to assume that she had not a care in the world. But the stricken look in her friend's eyes as she realized the unconscious betrayal in that bridal sketch had given Harriet a swift, shocking glimpse of a pain and despair that she had never suspected.

She wanted to help, to comfort . . . but she did not know the words. She was only guessing that Rae was breaking her heart over Andrew Preston . . . and as she did not like the man, thinking him pompous and arrogant and stuffy, it was difficult to understand that he could be so important to Rae. But the heart has its own reasons for the kind of loving that lasts and grows deeper through the years even when it has little or no encouragement.

'Is it very bad?' she asked gently and with concern.

Rae did not turn. Nor did she answer immediately. Then, with arms crossed tightly over her breast to assuage its ache, she said in a low voice: 'Bad enough.'

'I'm sorry,' Harriet said quietly.

Rae turned then, to meet the warm sympathy in those grey eyes. She smiled ruefully. 'So am I,' she said with feeling. 'Sorry to have wasted these years when I might have been with Andrew. All right, so I'm a big success — but fame and fortune are cold bedfellows, Harriet.' She sighed deeply — and then smiled in brave imitation of her usual cheerfulness. 'I only have myself to blame,' she said lightly. 'I chose a career instead of husband, home and family, after all!'

'Couldn't you have had both?' Harriet suggested sensibly.

'Probably . . . but I didn't think so at the time. I thought my talent would be stifled by domesticity and I suppose I didn't realize just how much I loved Andrew until it was too late. Oh, I was young and very silly . . . I expected him to dance to my tune and he was much too proud.'

'And now? You are both older and wiser . . . and you wouldn't have to work so hard at your career,' Harriet pointed out. 'It can't really be too late, Rae.'

Rae moved away from the window and began to tidy the big room. 'Yes, it is,' she said in a decisive tone. 'My life is here and Andrew is comfortably settled in Cashing. We've grown apart and we'd clash terribly if we tried to live together now . . . so we keep to our own paths and find happiness where we can.'

'It seems such a waste . . . '

Rae nodded. 'It is a waste,' she said

bleakly. 'Nothing matters but loving each other and being together . . . but I found that out too late to do anything about it. There have been other men for me and other women for Andrew . . . and I guess I'm not as important to him as he is to me. Men are so much more self-sufficient, aren't they?' She carefully plumped up a cushion and then tossed it carelessly on the floor and knelt on it while she gathered up the scattered magazines, all open at pages that displayed photographs of Lady Prudence alone or with friends or with her surprisingly handsome fiancé. 'He's nice, isn't he?' she said unexpectedly, pausing to study a particular photograph.

Harriet, busy at the other end of the room, looked up. 'Andrew . . . ?'

'No . . . this fellow — Guy Gunter. Nice underneath, I mean . . . not just nice to look at. You can tell by the way he looks at her . . . he really cares and it shows. Yet she isn't pretty and she hasn't any conversation and most people regard her as a terrible drag. It proves that he took the trouble to find out what kind of person she was underneath the gaucheness and shyness ... so he's a nice fellow.' She smiled a little enviously. 'She should be very happy with her *gentil parfait* knight.' She suddenly closed the magazine and threw it on to the pile. 'I hate weddings!' she declared brusquely — and not really meaning the words.

'You ought to be planning your own,' Harriet said firmly, marvelling that two people so obviously in love could allow pride to stand in the way of their happiness.

She knew all about the kind of pride that kept a woman from admitting that she loved a man who did not care in return. She understood the pride that urged a woman to pretend that someone else mattered when it seemed that anything was preferable to the humiliation of loving in the face of indifference. But she could not understand or accept that pride could survive when mutual love occupied the whole of two hearts . . . for how could there be room for that ugly seed?

'You've been reading romantic novels,' Rae said with a little, brittle laugh. 'Boy meets girl, boy loves girl, boy marries girl! Darling, it's a con trick . . . loving isn't so easy and marriage isn't the automatic prize for falling in love.'

'I know . . . ' Harriet said quietly, a shadow lurking in her grey eyes. 'Sometimes the boy is a married man.'

Rae swept on, unaware of the heartache in the quiet words: 'Even if they are both free it may be a long time before marriage is mentioned . . . longer still before they take the plunge! Things have changed . . . once upon a time, marriage was almost the only career that interested a girl — and she made a career of finding a husband and hanging on to him. These days marriage isn't a woman's reward for persistence but a relationship for both to enjoy.' She smiled suddenly. 'Sorry about the soap-box harangue — but I do want you to understand why I can't and won't rush into Andrew's arms and beg him to marry me. I love him — but I couldn't be the little woman sitting demurely at home thinking up tempting dishes for his dinner. Andrew's attitude to marriage is totally alien to mine . . . and I don't think that either of us is flexible enough to alter!'

'It must occur to you that he might marry someone else one day,' Harriet said quietly.

'Oh yes, it occurs to me . . . generally in the darkest hour before dawn,' Rae said lightly but a cold, cruel hand squeezed her heart at the threat that Harriet had put so openly into words.

'But you can't swallow your pride?'

'It's the size of a mountain after all this time,' Rae said dryly. 'Look, darling . . . you obviously don't understand so just accept, will you?' Her smile took the sting from the blunt words.

'But you don't deserve to be unhappy,' Harriet protested in concern.

'I was coping very well until I saw Andrew in Calderwick that day,' Rae reminisced, ruefully. 'Seeing him, even quarrelling with him in the old way, made me realize just how much I miss him. I've felt a bit unsettled ever since . . . but I'll get over it, you know. I always do . . . '

'I don't know how you can bear it — day after day!' Harriet exclaimed out of the terrible black despair in her own heart. 'Why, you don't see him for months on end! That must be worse than anything!' Yet, even as she spoke the words, she wondered if they were so true . . . for wouldn't it be easier for her if she never saw David again? To see him and to know that she had no right to love him and that there was absolutely no future for her love because he was a married man would be too much pain, she thought bleakly. Yet at the very thought of never seeing the smile in those blue eyes or hearing his voice or knowing even the briefest touch of his hand, her heart failed her and she felt sick and faint with despair.

'I can't wallow . . . I'm not made that way,' Rae returned briskly. 'I just get on with the business of living . . . and so does Andrew, apparently. But we've talked enough about me. What sort of a day have you had?'

'We've been really busy,' she said lightly, going into the kitchen to put on the kettle. She had meant to confide in Rae, feeling the desperate need to talk to someone who would understand and sympathize, but Rae had her own problem and her own unhappiness. Rae had loved for years and saw no satisfactory end to her particular rainbow and she had learned to come to terms with the situation. Harriet knew that she would also have to find her own solution to heartache — and a faint impulse was stirring deep in her mind. She stopped short at the sight of the sink filled with dirty coffee cups. 'Have you had a party?' she demanded, half-laughing.

'It looks like it, doesn't it?' Rae said, appearing in the doorway. 'I've had so many interruptions that I could have screamed! When I'm not working no one comes near me,' she went on in gross exaggeration. 'When I'm really up to my ears the whole world knocks on the door! That reminds me . . . Warren was here and he left some proofs for you . . . I think they must be on the sofa somewhere. Hold on!' She darted into the other room, swept aside the silks and satins that adorned the sofa and produced a slim folio with a cry of satisfaction.

Harriet opened the folio . . . and almost dropped it in astonishment. Warren had teased her into sitting for him one day, explaining that he had a new camera and wished to test it and she had agreed to please him while warning him that she was not very photogenic. She had not taken it very seriously and she had begun to be impatient long before he was satisfied for he was a dedicated photographer and could forget everything but his subject.

Skilful lighting, a love for his art and a gift for bringing out the best in people at the best possible moment had made Warren Hailey a very successful and popular photographer . . . and Harriet was a little awed by the quality of his work.

She did not recognize herself immediately in the lovely woman that the camera had caught . . . she would have denied in all sincerity that she possessed any degree of beauty and yet it was there in the wide eyes and the warm mouth and the lovely bones of face and head. Harriet was startled and disbelieving and then delighted, wondering what had brought about that glowing loveliness when she had always believed that she was blessed with very ordinary looks.

Rae had already seen the photographs. She had known Harriet too well and too long to see her as clearly as Warren who had an unerring eye for the quality of beauty but her immediate reaction had been that he had pictured her friend as she undoubtedly was, capturing the innate warmth and integrity and sweetness that was so much more than superficial good looks.

She knew, of course, the particular magic in those photographs . . . it was Harriet seen through the eyes of a lover and in some strange, mysterious way the camera had captured all that inspired him to love . . . and there was something in Harriet's expression in those photographs that convinced Rae that it was a mutual and very wonderful love.

'I'm looking forward to working on your wedding dress,' she said lightly. 'Something medieval for you, I think. No! Regency, of course . . . after all, Warren has met his Waterloo at last!'

Harriet turned swiftly, startled, about to deny indignantly that she had any intention of marrying Warren and to refute the likelihood that he seriously wished to marry her . . . but the words died on her lips. For last night, Warren had held her with a new kind of tenderness and she had sensed a loving that instinct alone had kept him from declaring. Perhaps he *was* thinking of marriage, she thought wonderingly. She was a newcomer to London but she had quickly found that marriage and Warren were generally believed to belong to different worlds. If she had been a very different kind of woman she might have thought it a particularly bright feather in her cap to bring such a man to thoughts of marriage ... and even though she doubted she could not help a spark of surprised flattery at Rae's confident assumption of Warren's intentions.

And if he *did* want to marry her? She asked the question of herself quickly, a little defensively, ignoring the instinctive protest of a heart that loved another man. Why shouldn't she marry him? Why shouldn't she accept the love and the protective concern of a man who had proved a very staunch friend and a dear companion?

For she had already made up her mind to crush her feeling for David into oblivion. There had never been very much future in loving him and now she knew that he already had a wife there was none at all!

11

It proved to be the last of Polly Prior's famous parties. Within a week, she was involved in a multiple car crash and taken to the nearest hospital in a critical condition.

David immediately left town to be with his mother. Polly had continued to regard Geraldine as a daughter despite the divorce and the two women had been close friends throughout the years. So as soon as Geraldine heard about the accident she promptly drove down to join David, to do what she could to help and to bear him company — and to comfort him when Polly died, two days later.

She had been too well-known, both as a writer and as a personality, for her untimely death to pass without mention by the national press. Harriet was shocked and very sad for David. She had been impressed by the closeness between him and his mother, so very obvious, and her warm heart was full of compassion for him at such a time. She had felt instinctively drawn to the woman who had such a wealth of good nature and warm personality and not only because she happened to be the mother of the man she loved. She had felt in some strange way that Polly Prior liked and approved of her and wished her well — and she wished that it had been possible to know her longer and better.

She hesitated to telephone at such a time but she ached to offer some evidence of her sympathy. So she wrote to him . . . and received in return a formal note of thanks signed by Geraldine Mellish. She did not know that David had not even seen her letter and she imagined that he had tossed it carelessly to his wife for attention . . . and she was hurt and a little annoyed, for it had been a difficult letter to write when she longed to pour out her love and the extent of her compassion and her desire to be with him and comfort him if she could.

Once again, she made up her mind to forget him, to ignore the fact that she loved him. As a married man he was obviously out of her reach — and in any case there was little doubt of his lack of interest. Whereas Warren's regard for her was quite unmistakable and a soothing balm for her bruised heart. She had foolishly tumbled into love with a man she scarcely knew . . . there was probably much more happiness to be found with someone like Warren, she told herself firmly.

It was humiliating to recall that she must have seemed to be throwing herself at David's head when she followed him down to the river . . . and it hurt to remember how kind and attentive and courteous he had been, how naturally he had taken her hand and tucked it into his arm, how warmly he had smiled and spoken and how convinced she had felt of a heart-warming and welcome affinity between them. There had been nothing of the married man in his attitude . . . at the same time, she could not reproach him with being too attentive. He had been warm, friendly, endearing . . . but there had been no hint of the lover in his manner or his attentions.

Having discovered that he had a wife — and such a beautiful, clever wife — Harriet understood why he had seemed to be relinquishing all claim to her, seemed to be handing her over to Warren with his blessing. It had hurt and angered her but now she knew it had been a tacit admission that he had no right to be interested or attracted where she was concerned, no right to compete with any man for her affections. Perhaps there had been a subtle reminder in Warren's attitude, she thought bleakly — or else she had betrayed a warmth of feeling that David was not free to reciprocate even if he were so inclined and so he had decided to make the situation plain.

Humiliated, hurt and deeply disappointed, she turned to Warren quite instinctively . . . and unconsciously encouraged him to love and want her even more and to suppose that he had been mistaken about her feeling for David — and when he asked her to marry him, as she had known that he would, she agreed. With unseemly haste, she thought wryly in retrospect, recalling her fear that the words would not pass her suddenly stiff lips. He had promptly presented her with the ring that he had confidently brought with him, an enormous diamond solitaire that weighed heavily on her hand — and weighed very much heavier on her heart and conscience.

Particularly when she discovered only the next day that David was not married at all . . .

Polly Prior's funeral was fully covered by an evening newspaper and referred to the writer's daughter-in-law, the well-known journalist . . . and Harriet did not realize that a young reporter had been confused by Geraldine's odd habit of describing herself as Mrs David Mellish.

But Rae was swift to realize . . . and swift to point out the mistake. Harriet glanced at her quickly, incredulously, a sudden coldness creeping into her veins. '*Aren't* they married?'

'Not any more,' Rae said decisively. 'They divorced years ago.'

'I didn't know . . . ' Harriet said slowly, twisting the heavy diamond ring on her finger and suddenly realizing the enormity of marrying a man when the man she really wanted was free to love and be loved, after all.

'Nor did that reporter, obviously,' Rae said dryly. 'I expect Geraldine gave that name . . . it's a silly little trick of hers! I don't really know why she does it — unless she's always regretted breaking with David and likes a constant reminder that they were once married.'

'She gave me the impression that she

was David's wife,' Harriet said quietly
. . . and a little bitterly for her meeting
with Geraldine Mellish had proved to
be a turning-point in her life. The
belief that David was married to the
beautiful journalist had persuaded her
to encourage Warren to propose and
she had accepted him in the firm
belief that it was wrong and futile to
want a married man. Now she knew
that David was not married — but it
was too late to want him for she had
promised to marry Warren and she
wore his ring and arrangements were
already being made for the wedding
— and she could not go back on her
word!

'Oh, you've met her,' Rae said in
blithe ignorance of her friend's bleak
despair. 'Well, it seems that she will
soon be David's wife again — or so
rumour has it. They've remained very
good friends since the divorce and it
seems that Polly's death has brought
them even closer.'

Harriet's heart plummeted to the

very depths. Despite her realization that a promise was a promise, she had still known a brief and blissful vision of a future in which David loved her just as much as she loved him — but the dream crumbled at Rae's words. She might just as well marry Warren and put an end to dreaming, she thought bleakly . . .

David mourned his mother very deeply for there had been much love and a real understanding between them in later years.

Again and again, his thoughts turned to Harriet and he knew how much he needed her . . . her smile, her quiet voice, the cool touch of her hand, simply her presence could provide a happiness and a peace of mind that no one else could bring to him. If he had doubted that he loved her, he did not doubt it now — and he knew how foolish it had been to suppose that he and Geraldine could really pick up the threads of a long-dead marriage.

He was a little irritated to discover

that various friends as well as the press were speculating on the possibility that Polly's death had brought about a reconciliation.

Geraldine realized that it was not the time to renew their discussion on re-marriage but it was very much in her mind and perhaps she quite unconsciously encouraged others to assume its likelihood.

She remembered that Polly had been very distressed by the divorce and, being a sentimentalist, she had often expressed the hope that they would get together again one day. Not recently, Geraldine admitted fairly . . . but perhaps it had remained a hope in her mind and heart despite the fact that both parties had always laughingly rejected the idea.

It seemed so very unlikely that Warren would ever want her, she thought bleakly. She was growing older and her looks would eventually fade and her friends would fall away as they became involved with homes and families and she would be even lonelier and entirely unfulfilled with only a somewhat empty career to show for the fact that she had lived at all. Unless she married David . . .

And then, the morning of the funeral, she saw the announcement of Warren's engagement to Harriet Burns in the newspapers . . . and some of the tears she shed that day were for the shattering of a long-cherished dream. She had always known in her heart that it was hopeless to love and want him and to cling to the foolish belief that one day he would realize where his happiness really lay . . . but one could not stifle every dream and that one had persisted throughout the years. While he had remained a confirmed bachelor with a string of light-hearted, meaningless affairs to his credit, she had been able to cherish her dream — but now he had met someone who really touched his heart and he meant to marry her and so Geraldine knew that her dream must end.

It was even more important to find a new meaning to life . . . and David's suggestion that they re-marry seemed more attractive with every passing day. She was lonely and the future seemed bleak — and David was almost as dear to her as Warren, after all. Perhaps they could make a success of a second marriage. Perhaps they ought to take this opportunity to find happiness with each other. Once, they had been sure that they loved . . . perhaps it was possible to recapture some of that joyous rapture which had swept them into a youthful marriage. It must be worthy of a try, she thought with growing conviction . . .

While David, unaware that Harriet had promised to marry his friend, grew more convinced that only a foolish, short-lived weakness had urged him to suggest that he and Geraldine should try again to make something of a life together — and it did not occur to him that she could be seriously considering the proposal. He knew that all his affection, all his understanding, all his concern for her could not compensate for the fact that he loved and wanted Harriet with every fibre of his being. He might not understand why it should be so . . . he only knew that she was the only woman for him and that he would stay single for the rest of his life if he could not have her rather than dedicate himself to any other woman . . .

David kept remembering that Polly had liked Harriet and wanted to know more of her . . . and that almost her last words to him as he kissed her before leaving the party that night had been about Harriet.

'Don't let her slip through your fingers,' Polly had said, smiling at him in intuitive understanding. 'That girl is pure gold, David — and you can have her if you really wish! Things are not always what they seem, you know.'

The words echoed in his mind during the first difficult days after her death. Had Polly been wiser than he knew? Had she sensed or seen something in

Harriet's behaviour that had escaped him? Had Harriet even hinted at a warm regard for him when she was talking to Polly during the evening?

Polly had been a clever, shrewd and very protective woman . . . and she would not have encouraged him in a fool's pursuit. She had known in a moment how he felt about Harriet . . . was it possible that she had been equally perceptive where Harriet was concerned? Had she seen through a seeming coldness, a seeming indifference to a warmth and a response that he had not suspected although he desired it with all his heart? A woman knew another woman so much more quickly than a man, after all . . . and his mother's intuition had often seemed to him to be a little uncanny.

Perhaps it had been a mistake to suppress the love and longing he felt for her simply because he felt that Warren was of greater importance to her. Perhaps he had been too quick to despair, too ready to suppose that she was indifferent. The more he thought about the little but precious time he had spent with Harriet, the more likely it seemed that he might have been blind and deaf to a certain encouragement in her eyes and smile and voice. It was very odd that finding himself so deeply in love should have shaken his confidence so badly, he thought wryly . . . but it was his first experience of a loving that dictated his every thought, his every emotion. He needed Harriet so much that he feared to reach out for her, dreading a rebuff . . . but faint heart entirely deserved his failure to win fair lady, he told himself dryly.

He realized that a woman must always be at a certain disadvantage . . . certainly a woman like Harriet who was so shy and unworldly and used to controlling and concealing her emotions. Rather than appear unbecomingly eager for his affection, she might have taken refuge in a reserve that he had mistakenly interpreted as coolness and indifference.

Perhaps it was all foolish optimism and certainly he had little foundation for supposing that she cared anything at all for him. But a man in love must snatch at any straw in the wind and, with his heart leaping with new hope, he decided that when he returned to town he would get in touch with Harriet. Her reaction to a suggestion that they meet must surely be some guide to her feeling for him!

He had been too involved with other matters to do more than glance at the headlines of a newspaper in recent days or to feel much interest in the social activities of his friends . . . and somehow it chanced that no one mentioned the news of Warren Hailey's engagement. Geraldine assumed that he knew of it, just as she did, and accepted the inevitable but did not feel that he wanted to discuss it — and as it was a painful subject for her, too, she made no mention of Warren or Harriet Burns or anything that might bring either of them to mind. And with her own heart becoming more and more sure of the wisdom of spending the rest of her life with David it seemed possible that everything was working out for the best.

She would do all she could to make him happy and to ease his longing for Harriet Burns — and in doing so she might be able to forget her own need for a man who had never really wanted her.

It was not until David spoke of selling Polly's beautiful house by the river that Geraldine felt that she could raise the matter of the proposal that she had carefully considered and decided to accept.

They stood on the terrace that overlooked the gardens that were very beautiful on that summer afternoon. In the near distance, the river was a silver ribbon as it wound its way dreamily through the sunlit countryside.

Polly had loved her home and there were some poignant memories of her for them both as they stood side by side at the top of the stone steps, having spent most of the day in making arrangements to close up the house for the time being. Then David spoke of putting it on the market.

Geraldine's heart leaped a little as she realized her opportunity. She tucked her hand into his arm said quietly: 'You wouldn't like to stay here, David? It's so beautiful — and I'm sure Polly meant you to make it your home eventually.'

'Polly meant to outlive me and everyone else,' he reminded her with a wry smile. He had not grasped any implication in her words and he went on: 'Yes, it's beautiful — and convenient to town. But I already have a house, Geraldine.' He smiled at her. 'My cottage in Calderwick . . . my dream.'

'You really mean to live there?' she asked slowly, a little dismayed.

He nodded. 'Yes, I do. I know a dream is often better anticipated than fulfilled but I can't give it up after all these years.'

'It can't possibly compare with this!' she exclaimed with a sweeping gesture that embraced their surroundings. She was deeply disappointed for she had always loved the house and, despite the sadness of the occasion, there had been a certain peace and contentment for her in the days she had spent with David — another little persuasion to seriously think of re-marrying him.

'Oh, Calderwick House has its own charm,' David said, smiling . . . but it crossed his mind that Harriet might not wish to return to her old home if the miracle ever happened and she was persuaded to marry him. If she should prefer to live elsewhere then she must have her way for he wanted no memories of her bleak past to intrude on their happiness . . .

But he had already made so many alterations to Calderwick House, alterations and improvements that he was sure she must approve, that she would scarcely know it for the same place. He did not mean even to hint to

Geraldine that he nursed such fragile and precious hopes for the future, of course.

So he added lightly: 'Anyway, this house is much too big for a bachelor.'

12

Geraldine was briefly silent. He could not have forgotten his words to her . . . no doubt she had seemed a little too determined to ridicule them and her subsequent silence must have convinced him that she did not mean to agree to his suggestion.

It was a slightly awkward situation for she had made up her mind to marry him — and it would not suit her at all to discover that he regretted his impulsive proposal and did not mean to repeat it.

She said lightly: 'Why not marry and fill it with children, darling David?'

He smiled . . . a smile that held a warm tenderness for the woman in his mind's eye rather than for the woman by his side. 'Why not?' he agreed. 'The thought had crossed my mind.'

Geraldine, assuming that they under-stood each other, felt swift relief. 'Polly would be so pleased,' she said softly, smiling at him with a new, warm confidence.

David was delighted by her seeming perception and understanding . . . and surprised into impulsive speech. 'Yes . . . she liked her so much! You knew it, too? I'm sure she hoped I would marry Harriet . . . she almost said as much!'

Geraldine struggled with a sense of shock and dismay. Then, pulling herself together, she said gently: 'David, I know you've had so many things on your mind lately. But do you really not know that she is going to marry Warren? They have been engaged for some days — and I believe that the wedding takes place at the end of next week.'

Looking at him, she saw that every vestige of colour had drained from his lean, handsome face and her heart ached for him as she saw the stunned disbelief and despair in his blue eyes. The stark exposure of a depth of feeling that she had not suspected was distressing and disconcerting and she hastily averted her eyes.

The words did not immediately register with him. It was just as though his mind refused to accept their meaning for that would mean a pain he did not feel he could bear. For some time, he had suspected that Harriet was in love with his friend . . . he had even believed himself prepared for their decision to marry and he had supposed himself resigned to the inevitable. But now he knew that hope did indeed spring eternal and that he had never really accepted the possibility that she could or would marry anyone but himself. He had recognized his love and his destiny almost at first sight — and he had been firmly convinced in the deepest part of his being that they belonged together and that Harriet must know it as surely as he did.

'You must be mistaken,' he said

slowly, refusing to accept such a death-blow to his hopes.

Geraldine shook her head. 'You haven't been reading the newspapers, David,' she said gently.

'No . . . no, I haven't', he agreed, a little grimly. His mouth tightened abruptly and a nerve began to throb in his lean cheek for there was a compassion in her eyes and voice that told him it was utterly useless to doubt that Harriet was entirely lost to him. 'So society loses its most eligible bachelor,' he said with a painful attempt at levity.

Geraldine said nothing. Instead, she put her arms about him and held him . . . and he stood stiff and unresisting and totally unresponsive in her embrace, staring over her head towards the water's edge where he had so recently walked and talked with his love and longed to speak of all that was in his heart . . .

He had planned to return to his flat in town that day and his heart had quickened a dozen times with the thought of seeing Harriet again in the very near future. Now it throbbed painfully in his breast with the knowledge that within days she would be the bride of another man ... and he knew that he could not bear to see her again until he had come to terms with his anguish and his sense of loss.

Meaning to drive to Calderwick, he parted with Geraldine on terms that implied affection and warm gratitude for all that she had done but gave no indication at all that she could look forward to a future spent with him. She was hurt and dismayed although she understood ... for once again a man had failed her — and at a time when she particularly needed a boost for her morale, she thought wryly. Now she must face Warren, newly engaged and looking forward to his swiftly-approaching wedding, without being able to flaunt the fact that David wanted her if he did not! She was thankful that she had never betrayed the way she felt about Warren to anyone . . . he certainly could not know and that was a small but essential comfort for a proud and sensitive woman.

Throughout the years, she had never ceased to love him or to want him . . . but she had learned that it was possible to live without him. It had been a blow to learn that he meant to marry another woman . . . but it was a threat she had faced for years and in a way it would be a relief when he was married and she could cease to dream. Dreams were for the very young, after all, she told herself . . . a woman in her thirties had to concentrate on living!

The next few days passed quickly . . . much too quickly for Harriet. She had made up her mind to marry Warren, to love him if she could, to be all that he could want in a wife — but as her wedding day approached she became more and more anxious about the future. For it was no easy thing to stifle her love and her yearning for David. She knew it was folly and a weakness to be despised — but she could not stop wanting him.

Geraldine Mellish was back in town but there was no sign of David and Harriet found it impossible to ask for news of him. It seemed likely that he was still involved with his mother's estate. Geraldine's return had not scotched the rumours that had been flying around . . . indeed, it seemed generally accepted now that she and David would soon be living together permanently once more.

Each time she saw Geraldine, Harriet could only realize more clearly that she was the kind of woman that David would obviously care for . . . beautiful, sophisticated, elegant, worldly and very personable and with a very similar background to his own. They must have a great deal in common. They must love each other . . . and that, of course, was the most important thing of all, Harriet thought bleakly.

She told herself that she ought to be a

happy woman. Warren was the dearest and kindest and most attentive of men. He loved her and he was eager for his bride and full of plans for her happiness in the future. He filled the flat with his flowers, showered her with gifts, treated her with every consideration and much tenderness — and only asked that she loved him a little in return. She did love him a little or she would never have agreed to marry him. During the weeks she had come to know him very well and to grow fond of him and to trust him implicitly — and if only she could love him as she loved David then she would be looking forward to a happiness beyond her wildest dreams

Warren had never allowed himself to question her willingness to marry him when he knew perfectly well that she did not love him. He loved Harriet and he wanted her on any terms . . . and in time she would learn to love him. He did not accept that she could really care for David. It was merely a brief infatuation, a passing fancy — and it must soon die for want of encouragement. After all, David had been the first eligible male to pay her any attention after all the years she had been virtually incarcerated with her mad old aunt, he told himself confidently . . . it was scarcely surprising if she had been swept off her feet a little. David had a great deal of charm as well as looks and personality . . . and more damage was done very often because he was quite unaware that women found it easy to fall in love with him. Warren was sure that his friend had not set out to capture Harriet's heart . . . no doubt he liked and admired Harriet as did almost every man who met her but he had never been in ardent pursuit of her nor given the impression that he was emotionally involved with her himself. So Warren had very little conscience in the matter. Harriet was younger than her years, naïve and inexperienced . . . she knew nothing at all about love. She would soon discover that her wishy-washy feeling for David had nothing to do with the heights and depths of loving that was marriage

Rae was intent on finishing her friend's wedding dress and her own, having cast herself in the role of bridesmaid . . . and it never once occurred to her that Harriet was not happy about the future she had chosen for herself. Any girl would be over the moon to have won a man like Warren Hailey, handsome and charming, well-born and wealthy and very successful in his career — and if she happened to love him then that was an extra bonus, thought Rae with the cynicism she had acquired with the years.

Obviously, Harriet was in love . . . she had virtually lived in Warren's pocket for weeks and he was a very attractive man, charming and persuasive, and he knew just how to coax a woman into loving him. He had finally found out about love for himself, Rae thought with faint satisfaction . . . and she was both thrilled and delighted that it was

Harriet who had broken through his defences.

It was all very romantic, she thought happily. No other man appeared to exist for Harriet — and that was characteristic of her for she had always known what was right for her and followed it through to the end. How many girls would stay in a quiet village to look after a cantankerous, demanding old lady while the precious years of youth slipped away? It might seem like weakness but anyone who knew Harriet could not doubt that it was her own particular strength that she was always true to her chosen course.

So she would not marry a man she did not love, Rae knew . . . and so surely did she know it that it was quite impossible for Harriet to talk freely to her friend, to admit the truth, to confess the doubt and desire and despair in her heart — and she badly needed a confidante in those difficult days.

Living a lie was abominable — but

she had committed herself and she must not hurt and disappoint Warren who had a right to happiness if only because he loved her so much more than she deserved. There was nothing to be gained by hurting him — and perhaps she would gain more than she knew by marrying him. Perhaps in time she would discover that this feeling for David, so persistent, so demanding, was really no more than a foolish fascination . . .

Rae knelt on the floor at Harriet's feet, her clever fingers busy with the hem of the heavy lace wedding gown that she had made to her own original and very lovely design.

'Only two more days,' she announced blithely. She sat back on her heels and smiled at the tall, very slender and luminously lovely Harriet. 'I really believe I'm more excited than you are!' she exclaimed in half-laughing reproach. 'How can you be so calm?'

Harriet mustered a smile but the fitting of her wedding dress brought it all so much nearer and so plainly emphasized the enormity of wearing it to marry a man she did not love that she was filled with a deep, dark depression. 'Aunt Sarah's training, perhaps,' she said as lightly as she could.

'It must be! Of course, I do feel personally responsible for the whole thing, you know,' Rae went on cheerfully. 'If I hadn't invited you to stay with me and if I hadn't been out when Warren came here that night you might not be marrying him in two days time!'

Harriet twisted the diamond ring on her finger. 'It's odd how things work out,' she said slowly.

'Always for the best, ducky,' Rae assured her confidently.

'Do you really think so?' Harriet asked, a little desperately. Could it be for the best that she had fallen so deeply in love with David only to suffer because of his indifference, his preference for another woman? Could it be for the best that she was planning to take Warren's love and loyalty and use it only as a balm for her aching heart and wounded pride?

Rae was busily arranging the hem of the dress to fall just right. 'What's the matter — cold feet?' she asked carelessly.

'Cold heart,' Harriet amended unhappily — and there was a wealth of regret in her low tone.

Rae's hands were suddenly stilled. She looked up quickly. 'You can't mean it . . . ' The expression on Harriet's face was unmistakable and she slowly scrambled to her feet, shocked, amazed and momentarily speechless.

Harriet swallowed. She was pale and agitated but quite sure that she must not risk Warren's happiness or her own peace of mind with the kind of marriage she had planned. 'I can't go through with it — but I don't know how to get out of it,' she said with a hint of panic. 'Haven't I left it too late, Rae?'

Rae turned away, biting her lip. 'Not

quite too late, thank goodness,' she said soberly. Abruptly she turned back, caught Harriet's hands and searched the pale, strained face intently. 'Are you *sure*?' she asked earnestly. 'This is just nerves, Harriet . . . everyone feels this way just before the wedding,' she swept on reassuringly, rubbing the cold hands and smiling into the troubled grey eyes. 'Of course you want to marry Warren . . . you love him!'

Harriet uttered a little sound that was half-sigh, half-sob. 'No, I don't. I love David Mellish,' she said simply . . . and it was a relief to unburden her heavy heart at last. 'So it would be very wrong to marry Warren, wouldn't it? It's just that I don't know what to do,' she added, a little helplessly.

Rae could not ignore that appeal. She spread her hands in a little gesture of defeat and then she smiled and said with matter-of-fact kindness 'The first thing is to get you out of that dress.'

Harriet stood still and silent while Rae's nimble fingers coped with the row of tiny pearl buttons which ran in an unbroken line from high neck to deep waist of the lovely dress. She stepped out of it carefully and Rae took it with tender, loving hands and laid it among the nest of tissue paper in the deep box.

'It's beautiful . . . I'm so sorry!' Harriet exclaimed with real regret for she knew just how much time and thought and loving labour had gone into the making of the dress.

'I don't have much luck with wedding gowns,' Rae said lightly. 'I made my own and never wore it. I'm beginning to feel a little anxious about Prudence Merrick!' She had meant no harm, no reproach, with the words. She had only hoped to bring something of a smile to Harriet's tense face.

Instead, to her dismay, Harriet burst into tears. Rae promptly realized that the control of days had finally and necessarily snapped . . . and left her to enjoy a good cry while she made some tea, her panacea for most ills.

When she returned with the tray, Harriet was drying her eyes and managed a rueful little smile for Rae. 'Feeling better?' Rae asked cheerfully.

Harriet nodded. 'I think so . . . ?'

'Still sure that you don't want to get married on Friday?' Rae prompted gently.

'Oh yes!'

Rae nodded. 'Then your next step is to tell Warren.'

'I know,' Harriet said bleakly.

'You can't afford to leave it any later than it is already,' Rae told her bluntly. 'Look, I have to say this, ducky . . . I thought you had more sense than to get so involved. Why did you promise to marry him if you didn't love him, Harriet?'

'It would take too long to explain,' she returned wearily. 'I thought it was the sensible thing to do, I suppose . . . and David never seemed to take much interest and then that woman definitely implied that they were still married and there didn't seem to be any point in hoping and . . . '

'Hold on!' Rae exclaimed. 'I think I've got a pretty clear idea of how it all happened. You are an idiot, Harriet! Why didn't you tell me that you fancied David? I could have done lots to help, you know . . . and I could certainly have put the record straight about Geraldine.'

'But it was you who first said that they were going to get married again!' Harriet protested defensively.

'I said it was rumoured,' Rae agreed. 'But if I'd known it mattered I'd have found out just how much truth there was in the rumour for you! As it turns out, it was just a rumour . . . Geraldine's back in town with a new man in tow.'

There was the sudden, swift radiance of hope in the grey eyes for Rae always seemed to know everything and she was seldom wrong. 'Truly?'

'Would I lie to you?' she demanded in mock indignation. She smiled suddenly with warm affection and understanding.

'So if it's David you want then you'd better set about getting him — but let Warren down lightly first, for heaven's sake!'

'You make it sound so easy,' Harriet said wryly but her heart was lifting with all the optimism of loving.

'Telling Warren is going to be damnably difficult,' Rae said bluntly, the warmth in her eyes taking the sting from the words. 'As for David — well, when a woman *really* wants a man she finds ways and means of getting him . . . '

13

Telling Warren was damnably difficult, just as Rae had prophesied. It was impossible to decide which might be the right moment for such a revelation . . . so Harriet simply took the plunge within minutes of his arrival at the flat that evening.

Rae had tactfully taken herself off to visit friends . . . but Harriet would have been very glad of her presence as she stumbled and stammered but eventually made a frowning, cold-eyed Warren understand that she was not going to marry him, after all.

He was furious . . . so furious that Harriet was alarmed by the savage look in his eyes and the bruising grip of his hand on her wrist.

'I shall be the laughing-stock of the town!' he said through clenched teeth, his eyes blazing. 'Do you know what you've done to me! Do you know, Harriet? Do you have the faintest idea of what it means to a man like me to be jilted at the last minute?'

She shrank from him, alarmed — but very swift to perceive that his first thought was for his pride rather than for the damage to his heart. She believed that he loved her . . . but now she could also believe with a thankful mind that it would not be so very long before he recovered from the blow of losing her.

'I'm so sorry,' she said unhappily. 'I didn't want it this way, Warren — truly I didn't!'

'It doesn't have to be this way!' he said roughly. 'I won't let you go, Harriet! I love you . . . ' He pulled her into his arms. She resisted but only for a moment and then she stood quietly but unyielding in his embrace. He kissed her fiercely — and her lips were cool and passive beneath his own. Abruptly the fire and the passion left him . . . and he laid his cheek against the pale, sweet-scented hair and sighed, once, deeply.

Then her arms held him and she pushed the thick wave of hair out of his shadowed eyes and she said softly, gently: 'I didn't want to hurt you. I tried not to hurt you. I seem to have been very stupid,' she added ruefully.

He put her away from him, gently but firmly, once more in control of himself and now more despairing than angry. She had never been lovelier or more endearing or more desirable than she was at this moment when he saw very clearly that she would never belong to him.

'David . . . ' he said quietly, a little bitterly.

Harriet had wondered that he did not ask the reason for her sudden change of heart. Now she realized that he had always known her feeling for David and that she had never deceived him and she felt shame that she should have stooped to this kind of foolish deception that had only hurt them both.

She said nothing. There did not seem to be anything she could say. And her silence was an admission he had not really needed.

'Does he know how you feel about him?' he asked stiffly.

'No . . . '

'And if he doesn't want to know?' he demanded roughly . . . and yet sure in his heart and mind that David could not fail to love this gentle, modest girl as much as he did. 'Will you come back to me, Harriet?' He was a proud man and it cost him a great deal to make that plea.

Harriet's heart smote her but weakness now would only make things worse. Although she had believed that she could marry him without love she knew now that it was impossible to fly in the face of her destiny. Perhaps she would never know David's love and never know fulfilment in a life spent with him — but she could never cease to love him or find happiness with any other man.

'How could I?' she said swiftly, almost passionately. 'You wouldn't want me if I did! How could you ever forget that it was David I really wanted?'

'I shall always want you,' he said quietly.

'I'm sorry . . . ' She stumbled on the words, her heart very full. Words were so inadequate . . . yet they had the power to destroy a man's happiness at a stroke.

He left her, knowing it was useless to plead . . . and his heart was very sore for it had been stirred more deeply by Harriet than by any other woman in his life. He would recover, of course. There would be other women. There could never be another Harriet . . . the lovely girl who, like Geraldine, had chosen to care for his closest friend and to hurt him almost beyond bearing.

Driving home, his thoughts went winging back to those light-hearted university days and the girl that Geraldine had been before life and living had hardened her and taught her to conceal her true nature behind a façade of sophistry. One could not recapture the past, of course, and these days it was difficult to catch a glimpse of the girl he had once loved in the mature and worldly Geraldine . . . but memory could still cause something to stir in the depths of his being, he realized with faint surprise.

Perhaps it was no more than reaction from the blow that Harriet had so unexpectedly dealt him but a man had his pride and the world must not know how badly he was hurt. He could not contemplate loving again for a long time, if ever — but he might find some ease for his heartache, some balm for his pride, some defence against the mockery of his world in a careless affair with a woman like Geraldine who had a light touch in such matters . . .

Harriet was packing when Rae returned . . . and she paused in the doorway of the bedroom, not really surprised but a little concerned.

'I suppose you must go,' she said wryly, knowing the answer.

Harriet nodded. 'I've stayed too long,' she returned bitterly. 'I should never have left the village, in fact. I'm out of my depth in your world, Rae. It's all so confusing. I prefer to be with people who say what they mean and mean what they say.'

Rae understood. It was very natural that Harriet should want to run away from the gossip and speculation of her broken engagement . . . and perhaps she was wise to return to the world she knew and where she felt comfortable. She was not suited to the fast pace, the sophistication, the modes and manners of modern living . . . and if she stayed she might lose the natural warmth and sweetness that was Harriet and adopt the veneer of pretension and sophistry that concealed the real nature of so many people in London.

'You're going home?' she asked

lightly, beginning to help with the packing of Harriet's cases. She had acquired so many new clothes in a few weeks that it was going to be difficult to get everything in!

'I haven't a home any more,' Harriet reminded her without self-pity. 'I'm going to Calderwick — but only for a day or two. I mean to look for a job and somewhere to live in Cashing. I can cope with Cashing, I think . . . but London is just a little too much for me!' She smiled ruefully. 'It will help that I've had some experience of working for a living at last . . . it was really very good of Clare to take on a green girl that she didn't even know,' she added warmly. 'Thanks to you, Rae . . . thanks for so many things. You've been marvellous!'

'I don't seem to have done very much at all,' Rae refuted wryly, thinking that Harriet had obviously been lost and bewildered and unhappy for weeks and that she had miserably failed her friend because she had been more concerned with her own growing conviction that Andrew meant more to her than career or fame or fortune or friends she had made since leaving home and the man she loved. 'I can do something now, though,' she said firmly. 'I'll get you away in the morning before the press vultures descend to pick your bones! I want to see my family, anyway.'

Harriet said quietly: 'Will you do one more thing, Rae . . . for yourself rather than for me?'

A little smile flickered about Rae's lips. 'Andrew . . . ?' she asked, a little dryly.

Harriet nodded. 'You mustn't let any more of your life be wasted!' she exclaimed warmly, vehemently. 'You know that he loves you and that must mean more than anything else in the world to a woman! Marry him, Rae . . . be happy! Nothing else matters!'

'It won't be easy,' Rae said slowly.

'How could it be easy when your whole happiness is at stake? But if you really love him then it won't be so very 'difficult,' Harriet said persuasively.

'He can only turn me down,' Rae said lightly but coldness touched her heart at the very thought. 'It would help if it was Leap Year . . . I'm not much in the way of asking men to marry me, you know.' She smiled at Harriet, a little impishly. 'But I might give it a try.'

Harriet regarded her for a moment with faint suspicion in her grey eyes. Then she said accusingly: 'You'd already made up your mind!'

'To see him — yes,' Rae admitted. 'As for the rest . . . well, I guess I'll play it by ear. But what about you, Harriet . . . what do you mean to do?'

'I've just explained . . . get a job and a room of sorts . . . '

'And David . . . ?' Rae interrupted bluntly.

Harriet was silent for a moment. Then she smiled and said lightly: 'Ask us both to your wedding . . . and *I'll* play it by ear!'

'That sounds suspiciously like black-mail to me,' Rae said, laughing . . .

* * *

It was a beautiful day. The bright sun dappled the tall trees with gold and fell warmly across the small, square house in its neat, flower-filled garden.

David gazed at the house — his house — from the window of his room in the pub across the road. Much had been done to it and he would soon be moving in. The days he had spent in the quiet village had quietened his unhappy heart and he believed that he could find a degree of contentment at Calderwick House despite the constant reminder of the girl who had once lived in it, the girl he had learned to love so very much, the girl who would be his friend's bride the very next day.

He stood at the window, regarding the house — but his thoughts were a long way from Calderwick at that moment.

A young woman came around the side of the house . . . a tall, slender woman in a linen dress, her pale hair gleaming in the sun, her warm, sun-kissed skin emphasized by the cool orange of her lipstick.

She lifted her hand to touch the leaves of the virginia creeper that grew so thickly about the quaint little porch that he had left for the sake of its character. Then she walked slowly down the garden path towards the gate, looking about her with a faint wistfulness in her expression.

David stared, not really believing what he saw, almost convinced that she could only be a figment of his imagination.

Swiftly he left the room and ran down the stairs and made his way to the front of the public house and stepped out into the sunshine . . . and then he stared across the road at the empty garden and the heart which had hammered with hope and delight seemed to stop abruptly.

Harriet rose from behind the thick hedge with the marmalade cat in her arms . . . and David breathed again. He strode swiftly across the road to the gate.

He smiled at her startled, incredulous face. 'May I introduce myself?' he said lightly, a little mischievously. 'I'm David Mellish . . . '

Duke was unceremoniously bundled to the ground and he stalked away with arched back and waving tail, deeply offended. Harriet smiled tremulously, happily and put both her hands out to David. 'I didn't know you were here,' she said simply.

He took and held her hands very tightly. For a moment he forgot everything but that he loved her and she was here with him . . . and then, as the soft, shy colour stole into her face and the thick lashes fell to veil the warm delight in her grey eyes he remembered — and he released her slim, oddly fragile hands.

'Are you alone?' he asked, a little

stiffly, looking around for Warren.

She nodded. 'Rae brought me down — but she's gone back to Cashing. She wants to see Andrew.'

'A flying visit?' he asked, smiling. 'A last look at your old home and the old way of life before you start on the new? I haven't seen you for some time but I'm up to date with all the news, you know.' He took her lightly by the elbow. 'Come and have a drink and then I'll take you over the house and you can tell me what you think of my alterations.'

Harriet was dismayed by the light and apparently untroubled reference to the engagement which he could not know to be broken . . . and would not feel that it affected him when he did know.

'I've been trespassing,' she said lightly. 'I've already explored the house . . . the back door was open. I thought the builders had gone for tea or something. I hope you don't mind, David.'

'Of course not! Well, what do you think? It's still recognizable, isn't it?' He sat her down at a table in the window of the saloon bar and went to get the drinks . . . and Harriet looked across at the house and wished with all her heart that she could look forward to it being her home once more. She had never expected to miss Calderwick House . . . and she knew perfectly well that she only wanted to return because it was going to be David's home and every fibre of her being protested that it should be her home, too.

He came back with the drinks and sat down facing her and his smile was very warm and friendly. Yet she fancied there was a certain restraint in the very blue eyes, a hint of sadness in their depths. Perhaps he was recalling that they had last met at the party just before the terrible accident which had taken his mother's life.

She touched his hand gently . . . and instantly his fingers curved to clasp her own. 'I'm sorry, David,' she said with warm sympathy. 'You must miss her very much.'

'Polly? Yes, I do,' he admitted quietly. 'She liked you, Harriet . . . she wanted me to take you to tea with her one day.'

'I should have enjoyed that,' Harriet said simply. 'She was very kind.'

David pressed the slim fingers and released them, reaching for his cigarettes. Harriet shook her head and he helped himself and snapped his lighter to life. 'How's Warren?' he asked, forcing himself to speak naturally. 'I must say that I'm most offended that he hasn't asked me to be best man!'

'The wedding is off,' Harriet said abruptly, staring through the window at the familiar village street.

'Postponed? Warren isn't ill, I hope?' he said quickly.

She was forced to look at him. 'I mean off,' she said as lightly as she could. 'I changed my mind, David.'

He drew deeply on his cigarette, his blue eyes very thoughtful as he considered her words. 'It seems that I'm not so up to date with the news as I thought,' he said slowly. 'When did this happen?'

'Everything happened very quickly . . . and none of it should have happened at all', Harriet said wryly. 'I told Warren last night that I couldn't marry him . . . he was very angry.'

'Angry . . . ?' David, like Harriet leaped on the reassuring implications of that reaction. 'I expect it hit him hard . . . but he'll get over it, you know,' he said comfortingly. 'He's very resilient. But how about you, Harriet? It can't have been very pleasant for you.'

'It was a mistake and I had to put it right,' she said firmly. 'I hate hurting people and I felt wretched about the whole business. But it had to be done.'

'You didn't feel that you wanted to get married, after all?' he probed gently.

'Not to Warren.'

'I thought you were very fond of him.'

'Did you?' she asked quickly, a little too quickly.

He leaned forward suddenly, his gaze compelling her own. 'Isn't that what you wanted me to think?'

Harriet picked up his slim gold lighter and began to turn it restlessly between her fingers, needing to gaze at something other than the warmth in his blue eyes that was filling her heart with glowing delight. Suddenly the end of the rainbow seemed very near . . . and the true gold of a lasting and very precious happiness was within her reach. Not fairy dust, after all . . . but the pure gold of a joy that came from loving and being loved to eternity and after . . .

'I'm not very clever when it comes to caring,' she said quietly. 'I seem to have said and done all the wrong things.'

'Perhaps you said and did the right things — but it was the wrong man,' David suggested softly. He took her hand and carried it to his lips, smiling at her with his heart in his eyes. 'I don't want you to be clever, Harriet. All I ask is that you care.'

She looked up then and her lovely eyes, so clear and honest, told him just how much she cared . . .

THE END